Prologue

Fallen...

Cast out. Stripped of all that she had, and all she once was, Sara plummets to earth, naked and screaming, from the greatest heights of existence.

Her body cuts like a knife through the clouds and on into the pitch black night sky below. The thin, frigid air whips harshly at her face, forcing tears from her eyes and choking off her screams. This is not the gentle feeling of soaring she has known all her life. It is neither wondrous nor graceful. No, this violent free fall forces her stomach into her throat and she experiences her first taste of bile. It's a disgusting and completely new sensation in every possible way. The same can be said of the overwhelming terror that has her firmly in its grip.

Blinking furiously against the wind, she spies the twinkling lights of an unknown city far below her. Those lights, as well as the city itself, are growing nearer at an exponential rate. Sara is very much aware that no human being could possibly survive a fall from this altitude.

No human being...

"Mortal..." a deep baritone voice booms inside her head. "You will be banished to a mortal life." Sara would almost laugh if she weren't on the verge of mind numbing panic.

A very short life it would seem.

The buildings of the city are becoming visible, towers of concrete and glass rushing towards her at a lethal speed. *Will it hurt?* She can't help but wonder. What does death mean... to one who was once immortal? She wishes she had more time to ponder this... but her time is up.

Father... please forgive me.

It's Sara's last thought, just before her body strikes the hard grey pavement, and everything in her existence goes black.

Chapter 1

A Most Unexpected Discovery

"What are you, stupid or something?" An extremely portly, bearded man is inexplicably shouting at Joseph Ross from across the coffee shop counter. The man's face is turning an alarming shade of red as he juts a large take out cup aggressively at Joseph. "How hard is it to get a fucking order right?"

Joseph takes a long, slow breath in order to stay calm. "I'm sorry sir. What's the problem?" He unconsciously straightens his apron which bears the logo of Java Jolt. The boast of their coffee giving its drinkers the ability to walk three feet above the ground has yet to be scientifically proven.

"What's the problem?! What's the problem?!" Mister red faced shouty guy repeats this back like some kind of enraged parrot. He then proceeds to stare angrily at Joseph, who still has no idea what he's so mad about. It would seem that the customer is under the mistaken impression that working as a barista imbues one with telepathic powers.

Joseph somehow manages to maintain a pleasant expression as he waits for the customer to continue.

"The PROBLEM is, I ordered a caramel latte, and this is some vanilla chai crap!"

Displaying remarkable self control, Joseph stops himself not only from rolling his eyes… but also from telling this man to shove his latte where the sun doesn't shine. "Uh, sir-" He begins to explain things calmly, now that he realizes exactly what happened. However, a woman in line behind the human cherry tomato interrupts him before he has a chance.

"Excuse me there, but I believe you took my cup by mistake." She says to the irate bearded man in a charming southern drawl.

Taking a closer look at the cup, he rotates it slowly in his hand, revealing the name Sheila written boldly on its side. Everyone turns their heads as one towards the pick up spot at the end of the counter. There sits a grande cup, tall and proud, bearing the name Norman. His caramel latte, eagerly awaiting the titillation of his big, bearded face suckling on its to-go lid.

Norman sputters. "Wha- Well you should have a better system so you're not always screwing things up like this. You can be damn sure your manager is going to hear about this in the morning."

Norman shoves Sheila's cup across the counter at Joseph before grabbing his caramel latte and storming out in an overly dramatic huff.

"God, what a dick!" Sheila offers, to which Joseph enjoys a much needed chuckle. Sheila is one of his regulars, a nurse at a nearby hospital who comes in every night on the way to the late shift.

"Sit tight, we'll get you a fresh one. I'm really sorry about that." He assures her with a grin.

"Hey, not your fault hon. You guys do a terrific job. Some of us sure do appreciate it." She pulls a five from her purse and drops it in the tip jar with a wink.

"Thank you very much. Jill will have it for you in a jiffy." He nods to his co-worker who is already putting the finishing touches on her vanilla chai latte. "Have a great night at work." He says with a genuine smile. Perhaps his best quality, it can always be said that Joseph is nothing if not genuine.

"Thanks hon." She gives him a friendly wave as Jill hands her the cup and she heads off.

Joseph has been working the evening shift at Java Jolt ever since the massive coffee mega-chain bought out McGowan's books. The quaint little bookshop had occupied this storefront since the eighties. Joseph worked for Mr. McGowan going on five years up until he was forced to close up shop for good. These days in particular, Joseph tends to stick with things that are familiar, things that are safe. A new business perhaps, a new job, yet he's still very much in the same place.

"It's all digital this, and download that!" Old Mr. McGowan had lamented to him repeatedly, as his livelihood of over thirty years slipped away. In the last year, Joseph even offered to take a severe pay cut to try to help the old man stay afloat. Mr. McGowan wouldn't hear of it of course. In fact, he still gave Joseph his annual raise even though he honestly couldn't afford it. His old boss likes to stop by once a week or so to visit. Joseph never charges him for his coffee. Mr. McGowan is forced to scrape by on a tiny military pension from his youth now, along with a couple other small financial nest eggs he had prepared. Any money he received from the sale of his store evaporated just by paying off his creditors.

"I'll start cleaning out the machines Joe, you have tables and garbage tonight." Jill informs him.

Although he has been there longer, Jill is the evening supervisor and his boss during the shift. Joseph has no great thirst for advancement in the Java Jolt empire.

"Right." He replies. Closing time is upon them, so he flips the open sign to closed and bolts the door.

Joseph is twenty-six years old, caught squarely between youth and maturity. He has light brown hair that rebelliously likes to turn wavy in wet weather. He usually keeps it cut fairly short, but recently he's let it grow out a bit more. It gives him that just out of bed look, which on him, looks good. He sports a light shadow of stubble, not in any attempt to be sexy, but rather from his aversion to shaving. Standing a hair over six feet tall, and in good shape, he is considered quite handsome. Maybe not Zoolander male model handsome, but an old time movie star kind of handsome.

His jaw is square and his eyes are set deeply beneath his brow. His nose is straight and sharp, giving him a strong profile. He has the sort of eyes that can go from darkly smoldering to soft and warm in a heartbeat. They are a cloudy green, almost grey, but in the right light can turn blue. He gets no shortage of glances from many a female patron... and a few from the men too. Several of his co-workers have flirted with him in his time here. He tries not to encourage it, but he doesn't put the kibosh on it either. The problem is, they are always a bit too far on the young side, nineteen, twenty, so he doesn't go there. At least that's what he likes to tell himself.

Joseph finishes wiping down the tables and mopping the floor. Putting the pail away, he gathers up all the bags of garbage from the day while Jill is still occupied flushing out and rinsing the machines. With autumn in full swing, the sun has set a while ago. An oppressive darkness greets Joseph as he opens the back door. There is a distinct chill in the air as he staggers his way out into the alley, juggling way too many trash bags. Joseph currently holds the record for most garbage bags to the dumpster in one trip. A very minor point of pride in his life.

He manages to waddle his way over to the bin and tosses the bags in one at a time. As he is throwing the last one, something catches his attention from the corner of his eye. A mysterious object, very pale, almost luminous in the moonlight. Whatever it is, it strikes a sharp contrast to the rest of the dark alley. Joseph peers, squinting, trying to make it out, but it's too far away. As it is, the thing is mostly blocked from his view by the next row of dumpsters.

His innate curiosity piqued, his feet begin to move, and he walks towards the other dumpsters. An unexplained chill runs down his spine and only increases the nearer he draws to the edge of the large bins. This chill has absolutely nothing to do with the fall air. With a gasp, he stops breathing completely, freezing in his tracks in front of the last bin. He can see now... the pale thing that caught his eye, the luminous object shining in the moonlight, are a pair of softly feminine legs sticking out into view.

"Oh God!"

If he had given himself a chance to think, he probably would have gone to get Jill before proceeding... but he doesn't, he just reacts and rushes in.

The delicate but shapely legs are bare, pallidly white, and completely still. Fear and shock make his heart feels like it's being crushed in a vice by the time he peers around the corner of the dumpster. Sprawled out awkwardly on the pavement, is a young woman. She makes no move nor sound whatsoever. Her long dark hair obscures her face and is splayed around her head like a silken halo.

"Shit!"

Kneeling down beside her, Joseph carefully brushes the hair from her face. Even under these circumstances he can't help but be struck by the beauty he beholds. He doesn't allow it to sway his focus. The first thing he does is place the back of one hand near her nose and mouth. "Oh thank God." He can't keep from exclaiming in relief when he feels her warm breath on his skin.

As soon as he places his fingers on her neck to find her pulse, the woman's eyelids open jarringly. She gasps and jerks away from Joseph's hand. Her wide eyes are filled with terror and confusion, her... lavender eyes.

Contacts? Joseph's brain automatically concludes. "It's okay! I'm not going to hurt you. You're safe. Don't worry. I'm going to call for help. You're going to be okay." He pulls his phone from his pocket.

"NO!" The woman screams.

"Calm down. I won't let anyone hurt you. I promise. We'll get an ambulance and-"

"No! No please. I can't! You don't understand! No one can help me. Oh lord. No one can help me. Please! I... I'm... oh Lord, I'm alive..." She begins to cry, and the tears run like rivers down her cheeks.

Joseph unties his apron and holds it out to her. "You must be freezing." He says shyly. The woman takes it and holds the inadequate fabric against her torso. "Listen, I really do have to call someone. I can't just leave you like this."

They both go quiet. For a time they stare silently into each other's eyes. Joseph can feel his pulse quickening. Those beautiful lavender eyes, call out to him, filled with need and fear. And yet, behind the fear, he also finds a wisdom, an innocence, a deep curiosity and maybe even trust.

In Joseph's green eyes, she finds kindness, integrity, a strong desire to help, and something else, something she can't seem to identify yet.

"Joe! What are you doing back here? You okay? Where are you?" Jill's voice calls out loudly from the back door of Java Jolt.

Panic immediately fills those lavender eyes again. "Don't! Please! No one can know. Please!" Her voice is frenzied and pleading.

Despite his better judgement Joseph does as she asks. "Yeah, I'm fine Jill. I'll be right there." He replies, then furrows his brow. "Okay. Look," He speaks furtively to the frightened woman. "I'll be right back. I won't tell anyone. I give you my word. Just wait here for me, please. Don't go anywhere." Joseph stands up and she nods vigorously. He does his best to act casual when he walks back to the coffee shop. Jill is standing at the door waiting for him.

"What were you doing over there? Taking a leak? Uh, we do have a bathroom here ya know." She gives him a smirk.

"Ha!" He tries to laugh. "No, no. I just... I saw a cat."

"Don't tell me, you're the type of person who takes in every stray you find?"

"Nah, I don't know. It's gone anyway." He slips past her through the doorway, hoping he can rush away again without rousing any more suspicion.

"Hey! And where's your apron?"

Crap!

He's forced to think fast. "Uh... it ripped when I was tossing out the garbage. So I threw it away."

Jill scrunches her face in doubt. She's a cute twenty-one year old working her way through college. She sometimes takes her position here a bit too seriously in Joseph's opinion. "Well you know we need to take that off your cheque."

"Yeah, that's fine." All Joseph wants is to grab his jacket, get out of there, and get back to the mystery woman in the alley.

"Okay then. I divided up the tips. Grab yours and you can take off."

"Thanks." He moves quickly to pick up his tip envelope from the manager's desk in the office. Then, grabbing his jacket from the break room, he dashes out the rear door in a far from subtle manner.

"Uh, g'bye?" Jill says sarcastically, but the door has already shut behind him and Joseph can't hear her.

He literally sprints back to where he left the enigmatic stranger. A part of him expects to find nothing there. Like the whole thing was some weird caffeine induced hallucination, just a phantom of his mind.

He clumsily skids to a halt at the edge of the dumpsters and looks down. Those stunning, huge, lavender eyes meet his once more. The fear that filled her face is immediately replaced by relief at the sight of him. This warms Joseph's heart and he has to catch his breath.

"I, uh... have a coat you can wear. Can you stand up?"

He reflexively reaches out to her. She doesn't hesitate, she takes the hand he offers and there is an unmistakable physical reaction from the very first touch. His heart flutters within his chest and butterflies dance in his stomach when he closes her hand in his. She allows Joseph to pull her up to her feet. His grip is strong on her ice cold skin and her hand trembles, but she likes the feeling of being held tightly by him. With her free hand, she tries her best to hold Joseph's apron against her naked body. Even in his grasp, she is extremely unsteady, her legs wobble and her knees bend. She's like a newborn fawn taking her first steps.

He wraps his black, mid-length coat around her shoulders. She inelegantly slips her arms into the sleeves as he buttons her up. Against his better angels, Joseph finds this action to be highly sensual, and he has to force certain thoughts from his head. Once she's covered up, the apron falls to the ground at her bare feet.

When the alluring stranger teeters again, Joseph puts his arms around the her. Her head finds a perfect resting spot on his shoulder, as if it were made just for her. Suddenly his heart is exploding like a fourth of July fireworks show, trying to break right out of his rib cage. He has to inhale deeply. Her dark brunette hair smells of honey and wild flowers and it reminds him of something from long ago, something beautiful, but he doesn't know what.

When she uses his strong arms to steady herself again, Joseph realizes his eyes are closed. Opening them, he asks her "Are you alright?" and moves to hold her upright by her shoulders.

She finds a sad smile, and the emotion of it hits Joseph like a freight train. "I'm... well, I guess I'm alive." She laughs softly. "I don't know if I'll ever be okay. I have far too much to pay for."

"Um, okay..." He has no idea what that might mean, but he does know that he will help this woman however he can. "We better go. You'll freeze to death out here."

"Go where?"

"Well, if you can't go to the hospital... Um... I suppose we have to... Uh... go to... my place." Joseph can barely get the words out. He can only imagine how it must sound. Telling a woman in distress, a naked woman in distress, that he wants to take her back to his place. He scans her face nervously, waiting for her to scream STRANGER DANGER or something.

Instead, she looks at him with trusting eyes, and says, "Okay."

"O... okay." He nods and puts an arm around her waist. "Then here we go."

With consideration to her bare feet and wobbly legs, he's careful not to rush her. Slowly, she is guided out of the dark alley and into the lights of Market Avenue. He feels her tension level rise noticeably and her breathing becomes fast and sharp. Joseph recognizes the beginnings of an anxiety attack.

"Don't worry, you're safe with me. Remember, I promised I wouldn't let anything hurt you."

"Yes." She replies falteringly. "Except no one can really promise that. It's only words. The kind of words an adult might use to comfort a child who is afraid of the dark, but I am no child." Then she adds, in a voice barely louder than a breath. "I am mortal."

"My car is just down the street, it's nothing fancy." His car, a canary yellow VW beetle from the previous century, is both a source of great pride and great embarrassment to him. It was purchased three years ago for five hundred dollars and an X-Box 360. It's been a struggle to keep the beast on the road ever since. From the moment Joseph saw it, he thought it was the coolest thing ever. Despite its severe rust rot and nearly alchemical procedure to start the engine, he still loves the old girl. He simply doesn't want anyone to see it, let alone ride in it if he can avoid it. Originally he had big plans of restoring the vintage auto. Now he's just happy if it gets him to and from work without crapping out.

"You can make it." He flashes her a supportive smile and thinks he spots a blush rise in her cheeks. The color is visibly returning to her skin as they walk together.

His meagre, reassuring words ease the tension in her body and she manages to find her feet. They reach his sorry little car with only a couple of curious glances from the passers by.

The passenger side door creaks horribly when he opens it. "Sorry." He helps her get into the car, making sure she doesn't bump her head in the process. She sits down on the duct tape covered upholstery and looks up at him. The interior smells a bit of gasoline. The last mechanic Joseph took it to said it was probably nothing to worry about.

"Thank you." She says, and he carefully closes the door for her. When he gets in the driver's side she gives him a weary smile. "I truly mean it. Thank you..?" She looks at him questioningly, waiting for him to catch her intent.

"Oh!" He exclaims. "Right, heh sorry. My name is Joseph, Joseph Ross." He gives her a great big smile. She smiles too and even laughs softly, and when she does, he could swear he hears music.

"Thank you Joseph. You are a very kind man."

He feels his own cheeks growing warm now. Flustered, he focuses on starting the car. Stage 1, put car in neutral with emergency brake engaged. Stage 2, slowly turn the key halfway around then back, then turn it all the way. Stage 3, hold key in position and fiddle with the clutch while pumping the gas three or four times, listening carefully to the sounds it makes, if any. Stage 4, turn the key back. Stage 5, floor the brake and clutch, while giving the key a hard crank.

With a bang, a groan, and a rattle of desperation, the engine chugs to life, sputters, then roars. "Heh, piece of cake." He looks over to see the stranger watching him with amusement. "You should buckle up."

She seems to be confused by this instruction, so he demonstrates and secures his own seat belt. She follows his lead and latches her own. "Oh yes, of course."

"Um, listen, you totally don't need to tell me if you don't want to... but may I ask your name? I'd like to be able to call you by your name, that's all." Joseph pulls out into traffic, avoiding looking over at his passenger.

There is only the slightest moment of hesitation, then that beautiful voice drifts like a melody into his ear. "Sara… my name is Sara."

* * * * * * * * * *

Chapter 2

The Night, Dark and Full of Terrors

The drive to Joseph's building is a short one and Sara spends the entire time gawking out the side window at the streets and the people who inhabit them. His apartment is in an old, four story walk-up which was built at the turn of the century. The narrow structure mimics a large brownstone, but without the actual brownstone, it's made from red brick. He parks his beetle in the small outdoor lot behind the building. After helping Sara out of the car, the pair make their way to the back door. She needs his arm firmly around her waist in order to safely navigate the concrete stairs. Meanwhile, Sara's arm rests snuggly around his shoulders. They hold onto each other like this all the way up to his fourth floor apartment. Sara raises no objections, she clings to him, welcoming his touch and his strength. The trek takes a very long time, but Joseph is patient and encouraging the whole way. Her legs jerk and wobble on each step and he almost wonders if she's never encountered stairs before. A ridiculous thought of course, and one that he scoffs at. Yet his mind is already running wild with all sorts of outlandish scenarios. He's bursting with questions about what could have possibly happened to her.

It's obvious that she's in some sort of trouble. Duh! You don't find a naked woman unconscious in an alley unless something pretty damn bad happened.

He tries his best to avoid thinking of the more disturbing possibilities. *Maybe some kind of head trauma?* He wonders.

He attempts to visually examine her without being too obvious about it. There are no clear signs of any sort of blow to the head. Although her long, naturally wavy hair could be covering almost anything. Other than being extremely anxious, she seems to be reasonably clear minded. Before he has a chance to ponder her general mental health, they arrive at his apartment door.

Suddenly Joseph is horror stricken. "Oh crap." He pulls his keys from his pocket. "Um, can you wait out here? Just for a minute. I'll be really fast. Okay?"

He leans her against the wall beside his door. "Okay." She nods, but she looks uncertain.

"You'll be fine. I'll be right back, I promise."

He unlocks the door, barely opening it wide enough to allow him to slip inside, then immediately shuts it again. Joseph's apartment is neither large nor luxurious, but the old building does hold some character. The doorways still have all the original wood mouldings, as do the ceilings. Dark stained hardwood baseboards ring every wall and give the space a much richer look than it might deserve. This place was built during a time when craftsmen took the time and effort to express themselves in their work. Back then, a building, an apartment, a home, were designed and constructed with care and vision. Not slapped together as quickly and cheaply as possible within what the law will allow.

The small entryway inside the apartment is flanked by a broom closet to the one side and another closet for coats and shoes on the other. To the right of the entrance is a short hallway which leads to the bedroom and bathroom. It takes only three steps and you're in the living room which is to the left, and is divided from the tiny kitchen by a narrow eat-in breakfast bar with a pair of stools for seating. In the living room sits Joseph's slightly ratty, brown and beige sofa snuggled up against the far wall. He has no end tables or lamps to spruce it up, only a sturdy looking coffee table at its feet. Each and every wall in the apartment is completely bare. There are no pictures anywhere, absolutely no decoration of any kind. This is in spite of the fact that the drywall is severely pock marked by numerous old nail holes.

Taking stock upon entering, Joseph is greeted by a familiar pile of empty pizza boxes on the floor beside the sofa. These are complemented by a platoon of spent Red Bull cans strewn across the coffee table. A couple t-shirts and a pair of socks are tossed on the back of the sofa for good measure, the less said about the kitchen, the better.

"Right, wonderful." He sighs and grumbles before diving in.

Balancing the empty cans expertly on top of the pizza boxes, he moves them to the kitchen counter and digs up some garbage bags. The boxes and cans go into one, then in the space of thirty seconds, another bag is filled by any assorted detritus found in the kitchen. The stuffed bags get hidden in the broom closet by the front door until he can take them down to the garbage. The stray dishes from the sink get deposited into the dishwasher. A hasty wipe down of the counter, sink, and stove is completed before he whisks the clothes from the back of the sofa. Moving like lightning, he makes for the hall opposite the living room.

Running to his bedroom, Joseph tosses the clothes into the laundry hamper along with a small pile from the bedroom floor. He does a quick check of the bedside table and chest of drawers for anything... inappropriate, let's say. Then he moves on to the bathroom. This room, thankfully, is already clean and tidy. Joseph needs only to replace the towels with fresh ones from the linen cabinet.

Scarcely more than two minutes after entering, he scans the apartment like a hawk, looking for anything he might have missed. Nothing jumps out at him, so he opens the door to the hallway.

"Is everything alright?" Sara asks nervously, still leaning against the wall.

"Yeah, sorry. I just had to straighten up a bit. I haven't had company in... well, not for a very long time. Come on in." As he reaches a hand to her, the door across the hall opens.

"Oh my goodness!" A tiny, elderly, African American woman stands in her doorway. She's wearing a night dress that could very easily be an antique, along with fuzzy pink slippers. The expression of exaggerated shock on the old woman's face is magnified tenfold by her eyeglasses, which would have looked dated back in the 70's.

"Oh, hello Mrs. Jackson." Joseph tries to sound pleasant and smile while thinking to himself, *Great, this is all I need.*

"You... have a new friend?" Mrs. Jackson narrows her eyes, glaring suspiciously.

"Yes, just a friend. Well it's late. Have a good night Mrs. Jackson." Joseph hustles Sara through the doorway, nearly shoving her into the apartment.

His neighbor's glower intensifies when she catches sight of Sara's bare feet. She begins to say something but Joseph quickly shuts the door behind him and can't make out her comments. He's certain it was nothing good.

"Sorry about that, she's harmless but she's nosey."

Sara says nothing, she's taking in his cramped apartment, surveying everything. She steps into his living room with trepidation, almost on tip toes. There is a large-ish flat screen TV sitting on a low console facing the sofa. The spartan-like lack of furniture carries over throughout the apartment. One might think that Joseph had just moved in, but in fact he's lived there for years.

"I know... it's not much." He fidgets and feels a deepening embarrassment at his modest lifestyle. Working the kinds of jobs he's worked, Joseph has never been able to afford any better. Not that money is Joseph's yardstick for success anyway. But in moments like this, it definitely bothers him, he can't deny it. The truth is, Sara is the first woman to see his apartment in three years.

"It's fine, really. This is wonderful of you... I just... I don't know what to do Joseph. I shouldn't have come here. I shouldn't have involved you. I was so stupid." She drops her head, putting a hand to her face.

"No. No Sara, hey, listen... we all go through bad stuff sometimes. That's exactly when you need someone to, you know, reach out and lend a hand."

She can't stop herself from grinning at this and she raises her head again. For a moment Joseph is utterly lost in the beauty of her smile, until it turns into a grimace of pain.

"Ow!" She picks one foot up off the floor.

It dawns on Joseph that she must have been in much more discomfort than she was letting on. "What!? What is it?"

"My foot…"

"Here, sit down." He helps her to the sofa while she favors her left foot.

"May I?" He asks, pointing at the injured appendage once she has taken a seat. She nods and purses her lips. Kneeling down in front of her, Joseph gingerly lifts her calf. Her eyes close and she breathes deeply as he carefully examines the bottom of her foot. At some point in their journey Sara cut her heel on something. Although there is almost no blood, the wound is dirty and looks painful. "Don't move." He orders, as he rests her foot on the coffee table.

After rushing to the bathroom, he returns with two wet washcloths and a first aid kit. He tells Sara to relax and lean back. She does as he says. Sitting on the coffee table, he faces her and places her foot in his lap. Cautiously, but meticulously, he cleans out the cut with the first washcloth, making sure not a single trace of dirt remains. Sara's breath catches a few times, and she can't help wincing even though Joseph is very gentle with her.

"Sorry, am I hurting you?"

"I'm okay." Sara opens her eyes and gives him a little nod. "Don't stop." She knits her brow and bites down on her lower lip again.

"I'm almost done." He assures her. Using the second unsoiled washcloth, he washes her entire foot clean. Then he applies some antiseptic ointment to the cut which causes Sara to jump and making a squeaking sound.

She giggles at her reaction. "It's cold!" They laugh out loud, and the shared release makes them both feel safer, closer, intimate...

Finally, Joseph tapes a square bandage over her heel and gives her a pat on the top of her foot. "Sorry, but I think you'll live." He jokes, trying to dispel the strange electricity hanging in the air. Although it's not so easy, especially after laying his hands on those long shapely legs. The heat of her soft, smooth skin is burnt into his fingertips. The way the rise and fall of her breast synced perfectly with his every touch was impossible to ignore. Not to mention the look he saw on her face whenever she would wince in pain. He could swear it was almost... sexual.

Of course, Joseph had seen ALL of her back in the alley when he first found her. But in the shock and adrenaline of the moment, the image of her naked body couldn't fully register in his mind. Now, here, with Sara leaning back into his couch... his hands still warmed from her bare skin... knowing she's wearing absolutely nothing beneath his coat... and his eyes tracing up her inner thigh, higher and higher...

Joseph stands up like a shot and proceeds to pace rapidly around the living room. Anything to shake those thoughts from his mind.

"So, you know, you can uh, stay here tonight if there's nowhere else to go. Then in the morning we can try to figure things out." He's wearing circles into the carpet in front of the TV, making Sara oscillate her head back and forth to follow him. "Um... are you hungry? I'm not sure what I have in the kitchen right now. Or do you need a shower or bath?"

Her eyes widen. "A bath?!"

"A bath? You want to take a bath?" He comes to a halt at last.

"Yes, please. May I?"

"Yeah, sure. You bet." He stands still and with her lavender eyes affixed on him his breath catches. "I'll uh, I'll just go get it ready for you."

She watches him disappear down the short hallway then hears the sound of running water. Looking down at her foot, she can still feel the heat of Joseph's hands on her skin. Her calf, her ankle, her foot, every spot he touched seems to tingle deliciously. So many unknown new sensations, and the mysterious feelings they stir within her.

The water stops and Joseph returns. "Can you walk?" He asks.

Sara nods but she holds a hand out to him. He helps her to her feet and they walk to the bathroom together, holding hands the entire way. She tries not to put too much weight on her left heel, but she feels steady with Joseph protectively at her side.

"So the towels are all clean. There's soap and shampoo, it's all guy stuff but... Oh! I set out fresh bandages for your foot when you finish, if you need me to help you with it..." He points a thumb towards the door. "I'll just be a whisper away." He instantly cringes at himself for that last line. He's sure it's got to be the creepiest thing Sara's ever heard.

"Thank you so much Joseph." She doesn't act creeped out in the least. If anything, it's very much the opposite. She smiles shyly, and as he softly releases her hand, Sara's fingers trail languidly across his palm, so reluctant they are to be bereft of his touch. And these two, who have barely just met, allow themselves a moment to just get lost in each others eyes. In this moment, it's as if nothing else exists in the universe. In this moment, it's as if they never want to look away.

Finally Joseph swallows hard despite a dry mouth and forces himself to turn. He walks out of the bathroom without a word. The door clacks loudly as it closes, Sara on one side, Joseph on the other, and they both take a long, deep breath.

He returns to the living room while Sara is left alone to struggle with the buttons of Joseph's coat. Her fingers, this skin she is in, the flesh and bone, it all feels so ungainly, so unfamiliar, like it's not really her. She looks up from her battle with the coat buttons and catches her reflection in the mirror.

At least I still look like me. Except for...

She nearly gives up on undoing the infernal buttons on her own and is about to call Joseph to help.

No! She tells herself adamantly. Not only does she need to learn to do these things for herself, but also, she suddenly feels strangely about Joseph seeing her naked.

Human modesty..? She wonders. *Or something else?*

When she eventually gets the coat undone, she hangs it up on a hook on the back of the bathroom door. Standing naked, she scrutinizes her form in the mirror, then turns to look at her back. A stab of pain pierces her heart when she sees two long vertical scars running down either shoulder blade. She tries to reach an arm behind her to feel the freshly healed wounds that permanently mark her body. Choking on a sob, she is forced to turn away. Sara knows she will shatter if she allows herself to think of all she has lost.

She moves to the tub and lowers herself into the hot water until her body is submerged up to her collarbone. In her previous existence, Sara loved the feeling of being purified in water. It's no different now, this body, it's muscles, the aches and pains, are instantly soothed by the warmth that envelopes her.

A soft knock on the door disturbs her. "Yes?" She calls out.

"Sorry." Joseph says as he opens the door a crack. "I got you some clothes. They're mine, so they'll be big on you, but you can just tighten up the drawstring on the shorts." His hand pops through the opening holding two articles of clothing. "I'll just drop them here."

"Thank you Joseph." She calls to him as the clothes fall to the floor. She's not sure why, but she likes to say his name. *Joseph.* Something in that simple word brings her comfort, and she so desperately needs comfort right now. The next second, a grim expression falls over her face. Her head arches back and Sara weeps. With overwhelming, soul shaking sobs, she exorcises the grief from her heart... if only for a time.

When Joseph hears the bathroom door open several minutes later, he jumps up from the sofa. Sara walks into the living room and he notices her legs are much steadier beneath her now. A new bandage is taped to her left heel to protect the cut she suffered. She's donned Joseph's Superman t-shirt which drapes over her body like a poorly fitted mini dress. Without a bra, Sara's breasts poke pointedly and noticeably at the blue and red top he lent her. She is almost half a foot shorter than Joseph, so his grey board shorts stretch down her legs, stopping in the middle of her calf. On her, they look like really, really, loose fitting capri pants.

"Feeling any better?"

"Yes Joseph. Thank you for the clothes." The look on her face doesn't come across like someone who is feeling better. "I need to leave." She announces abruptly.

"Oh." There is surprise and disappointment in his voice. "Do you have somewhere you can go?"

She wraps her arms protectively around herself but only shrugs in reply.

"Um... then do you have someone you can call to come get you? Friends, or family?"

She has to turn away from him at the mention of family. "I just can't stay. I can't let you get involved any further Joseph. I've already been so thoughtless, so irresponsible."

"Sara... you don't even have shoes." He takes a few tentative steps towards her. He's cautious, as he would be with a skittish animal, afraid that she might bolt. "I can't let you just... I mean, at least stay tonight. You're already here. If it's something with your boyfriend... or husband... if you can't go back home, there are places, you know, that help women in your situation."

She faces him again with a soft smile, touched by the depth of his kindness. "It's not about a man. It's nothing in the way you think. But no... I cannot go home." There is no smiling now. "I can never go home again."

"Then stay here tonight. I swear I won't try anything. You sleep in the bedroom and I'll sleep on the couch." He inches a little closer, within arms reach. Her head has dropped, her eyes cast to the floor while she argues with herself. "Sara." He places a hand under her chin and lifts it until she meets his gaze. "Let me help you."

Her nose sniffles. "Only tonight." She takes his outstretched hand tightly with both of hers. "I mean it. Only tonight. You have no idea of the danger I've placed you in."

"You could tell me..." He tilts his head to the side and raises his eyebrows in a gentle attempt to get her to open up.

"I'm sorry." She releases his hand and shakes her head.

"Okay." He nods. "Well, you must be ready to drop. The bedroom is the door opposite the bathroom." He gestures his thumb towards the hallway. "I changed the sheets while you were in the bath."

Sara doesn't say anything. She nods and turns, making her way to the bedroom.

"I'll be right out here if you need anything Sara."

"Thank you... Joseph." There is a shocking amount of emotion in her voice. Joseph holds his breath as he listens to hear the bedroom door close.

He turns from the hall and flops onto the sofa. Grabbing the remote, he turns on the TV and begins scrolling through the channel guide. *Rerun, rerun, neocon political channel masquerading as news, rerun, crappy movie, Aussie rules football...*

He can't be bothered to pick a show, his mind is too preoccupied by the beautiful woman sleeping in his bed. He leaves the TV on the local news just to have some background noise to distract his mind. His eyes are beginning to close anyway. His body is crashing as the earlier adrenaline rush wears off.

A female newscaster is on the screen, but whatever she is saying can't pierce the fog of Joseph's tired brain. However, a snippet of the news ticker on the bottom of the picture manages to stick. All Joseph sees before he drifts off to sleep are the words, **-killed in grisly attack by unidentified animal, police are on alert.**

Sara is standing motionless in the dark, but it's not like any natural type of darkness. This darkness is a thing, this darkness... is alive. She hears breathing, snuffling, snarling... and giggling. Her own breathing grows rapid and the sound of blood rushing through her veins is deafening in her ears. There is a sickening, coppery smell in the air. Waves of terror paralyze her. This thing is all around her, she is surrounded, there is no escape.

"You smell... like fear." A scratchy but almost child-like voice speaks from the dark. "A lost... little lamb..."

Sara flails about blindly in an attempt to feel her way to safety. This darkness is so all consuming that it's impossible to even see her own hands in front of her face. Panic takes her and she tries to run, but her feet can't move. They are caught, sunken into something black, strong, and unyielding.

"Little lamb... sent to... the slaughter?"

"Leave me alone!" Her scream is met by laughter. Taunting laughter coming from all around her.

"Oh... but I... owe you so much little lamb... little bird... fallen from your perch. Where are your wings little bird? Did you sin? Did you dare think for yourself? Have you opened your eyes, or did you let desire sway you?"

"No..." She gasps. She can't catch her breath, she fights to gulp air into her lungs. She knows that humans have a word for it but she can't think of it in the state she's in. "I only tried..." She croaks, "to help."

"Yesssssss, I know you did little bird, and now receive..." A pair of blood red, glowing eyes appear from the dark, along with two rows of silvery fangs. "...your reward."

Something heavy knocks Sara off her feet, pinning her down. Hot, foul smelling breath hits her in the face. It reeks of rot and death. Sharp claws pierce her abdomen and silvery fangs clamp onto her neck preventing her from screaming. *Oh Lord, no...* is all that she can think.

Then, in one horrible, violent, bloody motion, the dark creature tears Sara's throat out.

Joseph is jolted awake by a scream so blood curdling, he's certain someone must be getting murdered. It only takes him a second to realize that the screams are coming from his bedroom. Before he can think, he's on his feet and sprinting full out across the apartment. He bursts through the bedroom door. It slams against the wall and his shoulder crashes against the door frame. He turns on the lights.

Sara is sitting up in bed, her head is thrown back and her lavender eyes are immense, filled with horror. Her screams continue to reverberate around the room. Her hands thrash and claw at the air like she's fighting off an invisible attacker. The entirety of the picture is like something straight out of a scary movie.

"Sara!" He calls out, rushing to her side. "It's okay! Sara! Wake up!"

He grabs at her wrists, in part out of self defense, and also to try to rouse her from whatever nightmare she's trapped in. With his strong hands holding her fast, Sara's arms finally go still. The screaming stops and she starts to blink. Her breathing comes in quick, sharp, squeaking gulps, bordering on hyperventilation.

"Sara, can you hear me?"

She finally looks at him, but it is a lost sort of look, like her mind is returning from some far off place. Her body is trembling and she's soaked with sweat.

"Sara, you're okay. You're safe." He moves his hands to her shoulders.

"Joseph?" She asks groggily.

"Yes, it's me. Don't worry, it was just a nightmare."

"No. Oh Lord, no it wasn't." She shakes her head adamantly and balls her hands into fists so tightly that her fingers hurt.

"Yes, yes it was." He gives her a compassionate smile and gestures around the room. "See, nothing's here. You're perfectly safe."

Sara shakes her head again. "NO! I'm not safe, you're not safe, NO ONE is safe!"

Joseph gently cups her face in his hands and she chokes up. "Please Sara, tell me what happened to you. I'll help in any way I can... even if I don't really know what I could do."

"I'm sorry Joseph. You do not know what I am, and you do not know what I've done... my sin. I do not deserve your help, or your kindness."

"Don't say that. I can see that you're in trouble, but I can also see that you're a good person." He truly believes these words, foolish as that might be after only knowing her for a few hours.

A shadow seems to fall over Sara's face... even her lavender eyes darken. "Joseph, you have no idea what I am, I'm not a good person. I'm not a person at all."

"Sara, that doesn't make any se-"

He's is silenced when Sara puts her fingers to his lips. The look in her eyes is deadly serious.

"Joseph. I am an angel,"

His green eyes narrow and he scrutinizes her closely as she continues.

"...and I have become the doom of humanity."

* * * * * * * * *

Chapter 3

Welcome to existence

Maria Da Costa hates finishing work at 2am. The forty-six year old immigrant from Espirito Santo Brazil, has precious few options though. None, in fact. Life has forced her to work two jobs just to take care of her family. Her afternoons are spent pressing and ironing clothes at King's Dry Cleaning. After that, she rushes home to make dinner for her four kids. When Maria's husband died, she promised herself she'd do whatever she had to do for her children. Rodrigo got very sick very fast, and when their insurance company refused to pay for his treatment, the family fell deeply into debt. Regardless, Maria is determined to give her kids a chance at the kind of life she knows she'll never have for herself. That was why she and her husband moved here almost 20 years ago.

After dinner she helps the kids with their homework then kisses each one goodnight before leaving for her second job. They might protest and groan, but she absolutely will not leave until she gets a kiss.

Every mother thinks their kids are special, but Maria knows hers will change the world. Thomas is such a sensitive and imaginative boy, learning to play cello at ten years old. Little Catherine, having already skipped a grade, has a prestigious uptown private school offering her a spot for next year. If only she can figure out how to pay for it. Young Roberto has his problems. He's been getting into trouble lately, fighting, but that's not so unusual for a fourteen year old boy. Maria tells herself that she just needs to love him extra hard.

She has no other choice but to leave the children in the care of Andrew, her eldest, when she's at work. She worries for them every night. He is a responsible boy, but he is still a boy, not yet eighteen. They always occupy her thoughts while she works alone, cleaning this three story office building in the core of downtown. It's an area of town that few venture into after dark if they can avoid it.

Now at 2:16 am, after setting the building's security alarm, Maria leaves through the back service entrance. She faces a forty minute walk home. Any public transit that's still running doesn't go to her neighborhood. There have been many frightening moments during these walks. Gang kids have hassled her, sleazy assholes in cars will slow down to proposition her. Once she witnessed someone being savagely beaten by two men. Speaking poor English at the best of times and having no cell phone, Maria did not call the police. Terrified, all she could do was run home and kiss her babies as they slept.

Tonight Maria clutches her raincoat tightly closed against the unseasonably bitter night. It's not raining, but a forbidding cold still rattles her all the way to her bones. This night, the normally well lit alleyway behind the building is swallowed in darkness. She squints and starts to walk quickly towards the comparatively bright street in the distance.

She only makes it a few strides before being brought to a dead stop. "Querido Senhor..." She gasps.

As if melting out of the darkness itself, is some sort of hideous dog. This thing isn't like any dog, any animal, Maria has ever seen before. The beast is massive, with powerful haunches and very long silvery claws. The fur is shaggy and midnight black, yet somehow the beast stands out distinctly against the shadows from which it appeared. Its coat is wet and matted. Maria is certain that it's covered in dark, thick blood. There's a rotten and coppery odor assaulting her, causing her to gag. Then she sees the blood red eyes that seem to glow eerily, staring squarely at her.

When the dark beast bears its dripping fangs and snarls at her, Maria screams for help. She doesn't know if anyone will hear her, or if they would even care if they did. Turning, she runs for her life towards the far end of the alley, her only hope of escape from this nightmare creature. She's a slight woman, but a lifetime of gruelling work has taken its toll. Her knees strain and her feet hurt, but all she can think is that she needs to survive. She needs to get home. She needs to kiss her babies. While her own life is secondary, her children mean everything, and they have no one but her. She needs to know they will be alright. She needs to survive this night for them.

There's an unholy roar behind her. The sound of razor sharp claws scraping on pavement closes in on her swiftly... too swiftly. She knows she will not reach the street before this thing catches her. She knows it's hopeless. She knows she will never kiss her babies goodnight ever again.

Deus! Por favor Deus! She cries out in her mind and in her heart. *Meus bebes, por favor Deus!*

A deafening crash of thunder from the sparsely clouded sky causes Maria to stumble. She scrapes her chin hard on the asphalt and the wind is knocked out of her. By reflex she puts her hands over her head, lying utterly defenselessly on the ground. Maria can do nothing but wait for the creature's claws and teeth to tear into her.

A second passes, then another, and another... but nothing happens. It slowly dawns on her that the sound of claws on pavement is gone, there's no growling, no snarling, nothing. Holding her breath, she rolls over and blinks away the tears obscuring her vision.

There is someone else in the alleyway with her.

A man?

His back is to her. Whoever he is, he has broad shoulders, very broad, impossibly broad. The light is slowly returning to the alley, or else the darkness is retreating. As it does, Maria gets a proper glimpse of this man. Long, shining blond hair adorns his head. He is tall, standing at least six foot four. The man is clothed in a long black trench coat that wafts theatically in the breeze. In his right hand there is a long, thin sword, smeared with a vile, black substance. Most notably, his broad shoulders, which Maria had seen only in dark silhouette, become clearly visible in the light, but they are not shoulders at all...

They are wings.

Maria gapes in stunned silence. The light from the street lamps glint and sparkle off the two beautiful gilded wings. They unfurl, spreading wide, spanning nearly the entire width of the alley. The man in the trench coat rises slowly from the ground. He turns in mid air to face Maria. She is still sprawled on the ground, watching as the winged man runs his fingers down the length of his blade, leaving it spotless and gleaming. He slips the weapon inside his coat. She has never witnessed a more beautiful vision in her whole life, than this soldier of heaven, this magnificent servant of God.

Just before the angel soars into the night, he speaks. His voice is cold, like finely cut crystal, yet filled with a divine grace. "Beijar seus bebes. Kiss your babies Maria, you are blessed this night." Then he is gone, soaring into the sky at speeds belying physics.

"Obrigado meu anjo! Obrigado!" She kneels on the rough pavement. The pebbles dig into her skin but she takes no notice. Clasping her hands in front of her, Maria watches as the physical manifestation of her lifetime of faith disappears into the heavens. After tearfully thanking her saviour, she looks down at the spot where her angel had been standing. There is a large puddle of foul black ooze, the same ooze that had stained his sword. "Queime no inferno." Maria spits out, telling what's left of her dark pursuer to burn in hell.

Then Maria Da Costa, woman, mother, widow, mortal, rises with strength anew, and races home to kiss her babies goodnight.

* * *

"Listen Sara, you've obviously been through something pretty traumatic, you're exhausted. You just had a nightmare. I think you'll be thinking clearer in the morning after some rest."

That was the best and only response Joseph could come up with after Sara's emotional confession of her angelic status. He witnessed unmistakable hurt in her eyes when she saw that he didn't believe her. But how in the world could he possibly believe something like that?

Sara had only nodded in resignation and laid back down without another word, pulling the covers almost over her head. Joseph returned to the sofa where he proceeded to pass out at some point during the night from sheer fatigue. Now the morning sun is flooding through the open blinds in the living room and Joseph stirs with a groan, forcing his eyes open.

"Sara?" He mumbles.

"I'm sorry Joseph. I was..." She's caught tip toeing towards the front hall. "well... I was... sneaking away." Her dark eyebrows arch and she has an embarrassed grin.

"Sara, why?" He's hoarse and groggy, but his voice is tinged with emotion.

"You know why Joseph." Her grin disappears.

"Because I didn't believe you." He feels a stab of guilt and shame as he remembers the hurt in her eyes last night.

"No!" She looks stricken by this thought. "Oh Lord, Joseph no. I never, ever should have told you that. I keep making everything worse for everybody. That's why I need to go. I'm a pariah, if I stay here I will bring you nothing but pain and misery."

Joseph jumps up and goes to her. He's not a naturally forward person, but something in Sara has called out to him from the start. He grasps her hands and holds them both firmly. "I am NOT letting you go until I know you have somewhere to go. I'm not letting you leave here until I know you're safe." His normally affable manner has been replaced by an unbreakable determination as hard as steel. Sara, this chance encounter, has already changed him, brought something out in him. Everything in Joseph's manner tells her this is not open to negotiation and that refusal is not an option.

Sara is nearly breathless seeing this new intensity in his green eyes, there is a fire burning darkly there. She's unable to speak.

What is this? What do I do? Her mind races.

In the end, she allows Joseph to walk her to the sofa and sit her down. "Now," He releases her hands. "You need to eat something. I've got, um... peanut butter and... uh, that might be it. I haven't gone shopping this week."

Eat? She's been feeling an uncomfortable, empty feeling in the center of this unfamiliar body. An empty stomach? She wonders. "Okay, I'm sure that will be fine. Thank you." She feels a rush of warmth throughout her body when she sees his smile. Adorable dimples form in his ruggedly stubbled cheeks. *He's... beautiful.* She thinks, and knows that her cheeks must be bright red.

Sara sits quietly in the living room while Joseph runs to the kitchen and rummages through his cupboards. She still doesn't know what she should do.

I'm mortal. I'm exiled. Was I meant to simply die? Am I banished to wander the earth aimlessly, or is there a reason? Is there a purpose to any of this? What can I do? What should I do?

She has no answers, only questions. Sara glances at Joseph, still working away in the kitchen. In this moment, when she has nothing, when everything around her is frightening and uncertain, this stranger took her in... took her in and cared for her. He found her and made her feel safe and protected. Even though she knows he can't truly protect her, this trust she feels is so powerful. Her trust in him, Joseph. She doesn't want to lose it. She doesn't want to lose these burgeoning feelings. She doesn't want to lose... him.

Joseph turns and walks towards her. Sara watches his eyes very closely, they are soothing, calming, but also intense and smouldering. Then he smiles at her, and her heart feels like it's melting in her chest. She is made to wonder if this frail mortal body she now wears is defective.

"Are you okay?" He asks with some amusement. "I mean I know you're not really OKAY, okay... but you were staring. Is something on your mind?"

"Oh!" Sara realizes that she was indeed very blatantly staring at him. She feels her face and ears burning yet again, accompanying a feeling of... embarrassment? She's still fighting to pin down all these new emotions. "I'm sorry."

"Don't worry about it. Here ya go." He hands her a plate with a sandwich cut diagonally in two. "It's your lucky day. I had peanut butter AND Nutella!" He announces this with a great deal of exaggerated pride.

Even though Sara has no idea what it means, she can't help but giggle. "Thank you Joseph."

He tries to ignore the intense feelings she sparks in him every time she says his name. He knows full well, were he to look into her eyes for too long, he would be forever lost in the universe they hold.

He does not look away.

Sara looks nervous as she lifts the first half of the sandwich up to her mouth. With a less than graceful chomp, she takes a bite out of it and her eyes become huge saucers.

"This is...! Oh my Lord!" She talks with a fervent glee despite a mouth full of food. "Have you tasted this!?!" She holds the half a sandwich out to him.

Joseph chuckles a bit. "Uh, yeah. I have. I made it for you remember?" He smiles widely. He's beaming with a sort of happiness that he hasn't felt for far too long.

"It's so good! Take a bite!" She holds the sandwich right beneath his nose, almost threatening to cram it in his mouth. He laughs, but he soon realizes that she's serious, because she doesn't relent.

"Oh, uh... yeah. Okay." So, he takes a bite. His eyes stay focused on hers, those eyes that are unlike any he's seen before. A luminous shade of purple that he's sure are looking straight into his soul. There is something stirring so strongly within him, something he thought gone for good.

"It's amazing isn't it?" She gushes. She takes another big bite, then holds it out for him again. Joseph is famished so he takes another bite, while Sara absolutely glows watching him. The pair continue on like this. Sitting, staring into each other's eyes, feeding each other a peanut butter and Nutella sandwich. Both feeling an unspoken connection deepening, a special bond they can't understand yet.

As she swallows the last bite, Sara says, "You must be a very talented..." She searches for the right word. "chef!"

This makes Joseph guffaw heartily. "Oh God no Sara. Come on, anyone can make that. You're so funny!"

"Really?" She asks earnestly.

"Are you saying you've never had peanut butter before?" He asks, forgetting about her late night confession.

"I've never eaten before..." She says quietly.

"Right. Yeah, uh..." His memory is jogged and the air becomes awkward between them. "So I was thinking. I might know somewhere we can go for some help." This makes Sara's anxiety level rise. "Unless you want to try a doctor or something today?" He was hoping that by the morning her angel delusion would have passed. Sara shakes her head decisively at the mention of a doctor. He expected that. "Okay then, this place might be our safest option."

There's a slight tremor in her voice when she asks, "Where?"

Joseph tries to give her a reassuring smile as he answers. "Church."

About an hour later, the pair are walking the city streets. Before they could leave the apartment, there was a difficult moment when Sara described a kind of pressure in her lower body. Joseph asked if she needed to go to the bathroom and she looked ill at the idea.

After the sound of the toilet flushing, Sara emerged from the bathroom with an odd, half proud, half disgusted look on her face. Joseph has to concede, she is certainly committed to this whole angel thing.

They were forced to walk down to the church because Joseph's Beetle simply refused to start for him today. His turn to feel embarrassed, he fiddled with the key and the pedals for a good fifteen minutes before finally giving up. Sara was excessively kind about it, she could see how badly he felt. "I'd much rather walk." She told him, and put her hand on his arm. "I want to be able to see the world from down here at last. What better way than to walk among the people, see as they do." She smiled at him and instantly dispelled all the negativity in his heart.

She clomps along at Joseph's side in a pair of his Adidas runners. They had to tie up the laces as tightly as possible to keep them from falling off her feet. She's still wearing his Superman t-shirt, but he found a pair of sweats for her to wear. The cuffs had to be rolled up at her ankles to keep her from tripping on them as she walked. His pale blue windbreaker finishes the rather atrocious ensemble. Everything is way too big, making her look like a little kid who got into her daddy's closet. As they walk side by side in silence, Sara's eyes are repeatedly drawn to Joseph's hand swaying at his side. She is feeling a nearly overwhelming urge to take hold of it. She thinks back fondly to the way Joseph walked her to the bath, her hand in his. She remembers how everything in the world felt right in that brief moment.

To break the silence, she finally asks, "What do you think they can do for me at the church?"

"Honestly? I don't really know, but it can't hurt to get another perspective. We'll talk to Pastor Brook, just sort of feel things out. See how it goes. She's pretty cool." He gives Sara a quick glance. "Um... Listen Sara, about the angel thing, we probably shouldn't mention that. Not directly at least."

"Don't worry Joseph. I won't say a thing, but you know... the churches, mortals, they really don't understand the whole story of the Lord and the angels and heaven. It's all so muddled. It's all filtered through human self interest, preconceptions, misconceptions. It's been distorted over and over to suit the agendas of men. Any truth that once existed is so tangled up with misguided ideology that it's nearly impossible to separate the two. That's one of the things that has caused the angels to lose faith in..." She trails off when she sees the all too familiar look of doubt on Joseph's face and grows disheartened. "I... I don't want you to feel bad that you don't believe me Joseph. I don't blame you."

This unintentionally stings him. When they stop at a corner to wait for the WALK sign, he hedges. "It's not really that I don't believe you..." Sara shoots him a look that says *oh come on*. "It's just, I mean, that's like, really, really big Sara, massively, colossally, universally big! And I'm just a nobody, I work in a coffee shop, who am I? I'm sorry Sara. I don't even know if I believe in god, so to believe in angels..." He's not entirely sure what he's trying to say, but he knows it's coming out all wrong. When the light changes, they cross the street. "I'm someone who needs to be able to see things with my own eyes. If there isn't any proof of something, then I'm always going to question it. I can't just believe something unbelievable on the word of someone who read about it in some legend from two thousand years ago, and so on and so on… you know? I'll educate myself, investigate. So it's not exactly that I don't believe you, I just need to see it. I need some proof."

Sara bites her lip and thinks about that for a minute. "What about love?" She asks. "You can't see love, you can't touch it. Do you believe in love?"

This causes a marked change in Joseph. His posture goes rigid and he's suddenly defensive. Sara isn't sure what she said to cause this, but she instantly wishes she could take it back.

"Love is something you feel." He snarls through clenched teeth. "You can see it in someone's actions, you can see it in their eyes and... you can see when it's gone too." He sounds hurt and angry. "Believe me, you can see it."

Sara begins to reach for his hand, wanting to somehow take his pain away.

"We're here." He announces gruffly and she pulls her hand back quickly.

They come to a stop in front of a drab brick building. It looks more like a run down community center than a church, just a rectangle of beige with a few small windows covered by bars. There is no bell, no steeple, not even a cross on top. There is only a sign.

12th Street United Church
All are welcomed into the arms of God.

"Come on, the Pastor should be finishing her morning sermon." His voice has softened a bit but he is still not back to normal.

Not that I really know him well enough to know what's normal... Sara thinks.

They go through the open double doors and then the small lobby within. A woman's voice reverberates from the church hall. Lit by harsh fluorescent lights and a few small windows, it's hardly an opulent place of worship. Rows of wooden pews rest on a heavily worn red carpet. Every pew is empty, save for one. A lone man sits near the front of the hall. His clothes are filthy, as is his scraggly hair. Even at the back of the room, Joseph and Sara can smell something funky that they suspect is him. The man is listening intently to the Pastor, giving her his undivided attention.

Pastor Brook stands behind a simple podium on the slightly raised dais at the front of the hall. She is speaking of hope and redemption. The Pastor is skinny to the point of looking sickly. Her face is heavily lined and slightly jaundiced. Joseph happens to know she is only in her fifties, but she looks much older. However, her voice is strong and it booms in the small church.

"As long as you draw breath, you can be redeemed. God does not hold our failings against us. We are human. We will falter. God knows this. God only cares that you carry on, pick yourself up, and ask not only God for forgiveness, but yourself as well." She steps out from behind the podium as Sara and Joseph take a seat in the last row of pews. "Forgiveness." She continues while stalking down the aisle. She speaks directly to the man near the front. "God loves you. No matter your sins. No matter your mistakes."

Sara inadvertently lets out a sarcastic scoffing sound, causing the pastor to look her way. "God will forgive, if you are truly repentant. Redemption is the truest gift we have been given. When we fall, we know that we are still loved, we know that it is our heart that God judges, not our actions, so if you let God into your heart, he will cleanse your sins. We are never beyond redemption in God's eyes." She smiles brightly and clasps her hands together. "Thank you all for coming. I hope to see you again tomorrow, and on Sunday of course."

The pungent man shakes the pastor's hand and then shambles off. "Let's go talk to her." Joseph nudges Sara once the man has passed them. His voice is no longer strained, his dark mood seems to have passed. "Pastor Brook!" He calls to her as they make their way up the aisle. Sara shrinks behind Joseph but she follows him.

"Why, Joseph Ross! It's so good to see you. It's been ages. Are you going to be donating to our next auction? Your works always did so well for us."

He clears his throat uncomfortably. "Uh no pastor... I don't do that kind of stuff anymore." This exchange piques Sara's curiosity but she is too nervous to interrupt.

Pastor Brook eyes him with concern "Oh dear-" She clearly has more to say, but Joseph purposely cuts her off.

"Pastor Brook, I'd like you to meet someone. We're hoping you might be able to help her out, or at least offer some guidance." Joseph takes a step to the side, revealing Sara standing behind him. "Pastor Brook, this is Sara."

The small woman scans Sara's worried face, looking deeply into her eyes. A stunned expression falls over the pastor. She puts a hand to her mouth in shock and then slowly says,

"I... I know you."

* * * * * * * * * *

Chapter 4

Encounters

"Wait a minute! You two know each other?" Joseph's head ping-pongs back and forth between the two women like he's watching a tennis match.

"No!" Sara looks just as perplexed as he does. "That's impossible. I've never been... you know, here."

"Those eyes." Pastor Brook moves in closer, staring intently at Sara. "I could never forget those eyes."

Sara is speechless, unlike Joseph. "But, but, where did you meet her?" He's hopeful to learn anything about Sara's real identity.

"Ha!" The pastor laughs and a broad smile creases her wrinkled face. "Perhaps we should have a seat for that. We can speak in my office."

Sara feels a powerful urge to run, but Joseph puts a reassuring hand on the small of her back and nods to her. "It's okay." She could swear he can tell everything she's feeling, and instinctively knows how to make it better. She bites her lip and follows the pastor through a side door.

They end up in a small office with dark wood panelling. It's decorated with portraits of Jesus, framed bible scriptures and of course a large cross. There's an old desk that appears to have been bought second hand or possibly donated to the church. It has that public school teacher's look to it. Very industrial and well used. The two old, moulded plastic chairs in front of it share the same aesthetic. The pastor offers Sara and Joseph a seat in those chairs as she sits down behind her desk.

"I'm very sorry pastor, but there really is no way we could have met." Sara reiterates as she sits down.

"Let me explain." She makes a placating gesture with her hand. "Now Joseph, I'm not sure how much you know about me, but safe to say, I was far less than saintly for the most of my life. I only let God into my heart about fifteen years ago." Joseph fidgets a bit, he really didn't come here for a sermon or to hear the pastor's life story. He keeps his patience though and allows her continue.

"Yes, I had a very troubled life, lots of booze, living on the streets, crime, and a very serious drug problem. I started out just partying, being stupid, getting drunk, getting stoned. Then I hit heroin, and any remaining semblance of a real life was gone. None of this is a secret of course, I share it all in my sermons."

Was Sara in rehab with her? Joseph's overactive imagination goes to work again. Both he and Sara are wondering where exactly the pastor is going with this.

"Now that was when I really spiraled. I'd steal, rob people, turn tricks, anything I had to do to stay high. I'd hit about as rock bottom as a soul could. There was this dealer I'd mule for sometimes. I stole a shipment from him. I ran, I hid. Squatting in some abandoned building, I was shooting heroin and smoking crack for maybe two days straight..." She blinks rapidly behind rectangular eyeglasses, needing to pause and take a slow breath to calm herself. "I OD'ed. Laying in filth and squalor, my body and soul said, no more." Her eyes turn up toward the ceiling. "I saw myself. From... somewhere above, I looked down and I saw myself. My body was shriveled, pathetic, skeletal. My eyes were open, but they looked dead... Well, of course, I WAS dead. And then..." She looks back at Sara. "Then I was somewhere else."

Now Sara feels the shock of comprehension. "Oh Lord..."

"Yes, yes, it was warm and bright and safe. I saw so many faces, there were voices, I heard music, and I saw you..." The pastor points to Sara. "those eyes. I could never forget how they shone. Then another told me, in a voice like a beautiful song, that it wasn't my time yet, that I was blessed and that I had to fight. He said that my road was hard, but I had to fight and never give up. I could not surrender to fear and pain. I was told that I had worth and that I still had much to give the world before it was my time to move on." Tears well up and the pastor chokes back a sob. "I never gave up." She shakes her head defiantly, raising her hands to heaven. "I fought. I fought, and I gave, and I still give to the world."

Sara nods. "You were returned. A second chance."

"Yes. A blessing. I survived, I cleaned myself up. I lived and I still live for God now and use my story to help others find the way."

Joseph is sitting with a very lost look on his face. His plan in bringing Sara here was to dispel her idea that she's an angel, not to reinforce it. "I'm sorry pastor, but what exactly are you trying to say? Where did you see her?"

"Oh Joseph." She laughs. "I was in heaven. Or at the gates... I'm not sure. But she was there, so beautiful, an angel, and now you're here..." Joseph is all but forgotten as pastor Brook gives her full attention to Sara. "you have come with a message for me? Or a calling from heaven... I'm humbled... I will do anything. Were you sent to me? Sent to help us?"

"No." Sara replies quietly, shaking her head. "I wasn't sent. I'm... I'm fallen." This comes out as only a whisper.

"Excuse me dear? I couldn't hear you."

"I'm fallen. I'm exiled from heaven." She turns to Joseph at her side. "I'm so sorry I didn't tell you everything. I was so ashamed Joseph... and when you didn't believe me..."

"Wait a minute." He puts a hand up. "You're both honestly saying to me that you're... that she's an angel. Like, with halos and wings and everything. For real?" Sara flinches at the mention of wings. "Pastor... you honestly believe she's an angel?"

"I'm NOT an angel!" Sara cuts in harshly. "That's what I'm telling you. I betrayed the most sacred gift the Lord gave to humankind and so was I cast out by my own father. My wings were torn from my back! My very divinity torn from me! I am human now. Mortal. As mortal as you." Sara's hands are balled into fists. Anger, pain, hopelessness, fear, shame, so many feelings assault her. "I'm mortal. Lord forgive me... Lord forgive me."

"I'm afraid I can't help you." Pastor Brook says in an icily unfeeling tone. "I think you should leave now."

"What?" Joseph is taken aback by her sudden change in attitude.

"She has no place here. Please leave."

Sara's head drops but she rises to leave. Joseph does not move, he is staring at the pastor, anger rising within him.

"Joseph, it's alright. Let's just leave." She reaches a hand to him. She knows he is close to exploding, she can feel his need to protect her, to be her champion. "Please Joseph. Take my hand." Her soft, plaintive voice is able to calm the beast raging in his chest. He takes her hand and stands up. They begin to walk out of the office, but Joseph can't go silently.

"All are welcomed into the arms of God huh? A nice idea, but I guess you forgot to put an asterisk on your sign out front." He says with an impressive level of restraint and control. The pastor says nothing and Sara pulls Joseph with her. They get out of the church and he swears very loudly, releasing some of the rage he was holding in. "Aaaah! I can't believe her! Who does she think she is?!"

"It's okay Joseph. I should have known better, I am not to be helped. I am meant to suffer... that's the point of all of this. I need to serve my penance. You should leave me. You shouldn't be helping me."

"Fuck Sara! Stop that!" He takes her by the arms and his face is extremely close to hers. He is angry, but he doesn't frighten her in the slightest. She can see there is strength and control in his eyes. "Listen to me carefully. I am not leaving you Sara. It's my choice to help you." The strength in his hands seem to emphasise each word and radiates through her body. "Never tell me to leave you again. Maybe I can't stop you from leaving me, but until you're safe, until you can take care of yourself, I'm going to keep on helping you. I'm going to stand by you until the end. Is that clear?"

She's left paralyzed by the blazing heat flowing off of him. That fire she had glimpsed only in passing is threatening to become an inferno. She's not sure if she's breathing, she is transfixed. Her lip is quivering, her heart is aching. It feels like her entire body is being magnetically pulled towards him.

But his hands release her, he takes a step back, and the moment slips away. Rubbing the back of his neck, Joseph takes a deep breath. Sara resumes breathing as well. She feels dizzy, weightless, like she's floating.

"I'm sorry Sara. I shouldn't have grabbed you. Are you okay?" She is still unable to speak but offers a head bob as he continues. "Come on. Let's get out of here."

"W-where?" She stammers.

"Shopping I guess. You can't wear my clothes forever."

He dearly wishes he could afford to drape Sara in only the finest of clothes. Give her that whole Pretty Woman shopping spree. But the reality of his life means a trip to Wal-Mart instead. For a mere employee of Java Jolt, fine fabrics and high end fashion are well beyond his means.

Even at discount, sweat shop prices, he has to carefully calculate every dollar in his head. He's embarrassed each time he needs to tell Sara that something is too expensive. She's perfectly nice about it, incredibly gracious about it, but the male ego is what it is. In the end, he helps her pick out one pair of shoes, two pairs of pants, and three shirts. When she saw a pink t-shirt with a Supergirl S on it, her eyes lit up. "We can match!" She exclaimed with glee.

Of course he got it for her.

Assisting her with choosing underwear drew some curious looks from the other shoppers. For some reason Joseph felt completely at ease about it. It didn't feel strange, he wasn't self conscious. The only thing that mattered to him was taking care of Sara.

As for Sara, she behaved as if all of this was brand new to her. She would touch everything and giggle and show it to Joseph, and he loved it. He loves to see her smile, he loves making her happy.

They also swung by the grocery section and stocked up. Adding the food on top of the clothes meant that their shopping trip pretty much emptied out Joseph's bank account. He made sure not to let the stress it was causing him show. Seeing the light in her eyes and the smile on her face made it all worthwhile.

The joys of living paycheck to paycheck. He thinks to himself, but he keeps smiling as they walk out of the store, laden with bags. For Sara, he would do anything. As crazy as it sounds after knowing her for just one night, he truly feels that way. He'll do whatever he needs to do for her.

They stop outside and Sara changes into her new shoes and puts Joseph's borrowed sneakers into one of the bags. "Thank you Joseph. I swear I'll find some way to repay you."

He shrugs humbly. "Don't worry about it Sara. We better get this food back to my place before it spoils, and I need to work later."

"Oh okay."

Sara has watched humanity all through her existence. Although these firsthand mortal experiences are new for her, she does understand how human society runs. She's well aware of money and jobs and all these things. It's just that such things were always beneath her... literally. Now to be in the midst of it, affected by it, it's suddenly so very real. In heaven the angels would look down and tut-tut at the mortals for placing so much value on money. They would disparage human greed and their petty love of material things. Having to worry about finding food or clothing or shelter... those are things the angels simply cannot comprehend.

As she looks at the smile on Joseph's face, Sara is deeply humbled. She feels ashamed of her old ways. She realizes, in all the centuries that she watched humans, she never truly saw them.

"Joseph, I don't ever wish to be a burden upon you."

"Sara..." He flashes her a grin that oozes charm. "What did I tell you before? I'm helping you because I choose to help. There is no burden. None." That's not completely true and Sara knows it, but she still feels better for hearing it.

They walk in contented silence the rest of the way to his apartment. Sara takes in the city, the world, with brand new eyes. When they get home she has no trouble climbing the stairs on her own, even racing Joseph up the last flight. Reaching his apartment, Joseph juggles the bags as he digs his keys from a pocket. Sara giggles watching him.

Like a hallway ninja, Mrs. Jackson appears in her doorway silently, without warning. "Your friend is staying with you Joseph?" She's examining Sara with suspicion again, as though she expects the demure young woman to rob her in her sleep.

"Oh, hi Mrs. Jackson. Um, yeah, for a few days. She's new in town... so until she can find a place..."

Mrs. Jackson gives him a disapproving "hmm" sound and scowls. Her glower power is in full effect.

"It's very nice to meet you Mrs. Jackson, I'm sorry I didn't introduce myself last night. My name is Sara." She marches right up to the elderly woman and adjusts her bags so she can extend a hand in greeting. This catches Mrs. Jackson off guard and she meekly shakes Sara's hand. "I'll make sure not to do anything that might disturb you while I'm here."

"Hmm... well, thank you." She's studying Sara with curiosity now. "Now child... what color are your eyes..?"

"Oh!" Joseph interrupts. "Those are colored contacts... nice aren't they?" He has his key in the lock and is rushing to get his door opened.

"Hmm..." Mrs. Jackson isn't ready to relent yet. "And why on earth were you in your bare feet last night?"

"She was mugged by some kids on the way here! They took her shoes and bags." Joseph interjects again. The door is open and he comes over to try to pry Sara away.

Mrs. Jackson's attitude changes instantly. "Oh you poor dear!" She gasps. "They didn't hurt you did they? I keep saying, I don't know what's happened to this world, let alone this neighborhood. A woman isn't safe anywhere. No wonder you looked so scared last night. Are you okay dear?"

"I'm okay now, thanks to Joseph. He's a very good man."

"Oh yes... just needs to get himself together that's all." The old woman has a hearty laugh at this.

"Uh, I really didn't do anything." He laughs uncomfortably. "Come on Sara, we need to get these groceries put away." He tries to pull her with him.

"Now you come over and have tea with me while you're here dearie." Mrs. Jackson is wearing a big, welcoming smile now.

"If she has time." Joseph cuts in yet again. "Have a nice day Mrs. Jackson." He pushes Sara through the apartment door and closes it behind them.

Sara says, "She's nice!"

"Yeah, maybe, but she could teach the CIA a thing or two about interrogation. We need to be careful Sara."

"I felt bad that we lied to her." She pouts, following him into the kitchen. They place the grocery bags on the counter.

"I know Sara, but we have no choice. We can't tell people... you know... the truth. Today proved that."

"You still don't believe me, do you?"

Joseph goes still, he can't look at her. "I can put away the groceries. Why don't you go change into your new clothes."

"Okay." She replies sadly. Carrying the bags of clothing to the bedroom, she closes the door.

"Sara." A voice says plainly from inside the room.

She nearly jumps out of her skin and drops the bags to the floor. In front of the bed stands a tall man in a black trench coat that nearly brushes the floor. His hair is long and could have been spun from pure sunlight. Folded tightly to his back are two glittering golden wings.

"Julian!" Sara exclaims very loudly, then covers her mouth with her hand, terrified that Joseph might come to investigate.

"You need not worry Sara. I am ensuring that the mortal cannot hear us." His face is inscrutable, neither angry nor pleasant. It holds an angelic detachment which Sara is all too familiar with.

His features are stunning. An aquiline nose and strong cheekbones compliment a sculpted brow, masculine jaw and ice blue eyes. By human or angelic standards, Julian is a visual masterpiece. Sara has always been awed by his beauty.

"What are you doing here Julian? HOW can you be here? It's not possible!" Despite his previous assurance, Sara still tries her best to speak softly.

He moves nearer. "Because of you of course Sara. You broke the boundary. The balance is no more. The seals are gone. Earth, humanity, all will once again become hell's playground. This time, with no possible way to close the doors... Sara, do you even comprehend what you have done?"

"By the Lord! Do you think I don't know? Is that why you've come? To torture me... torment me?" She is no longer able to keep her voice down. Her face is twisted by pain and despair.

Julian sighs. "What are you doing with that mortal?" His voice drips with disdain and he juts his chin at the bedroom door behind her.

Sara feels ashamed by the question although she doesn't know why. Her arms unconsciously wrap around herself protectively. "Joseph? He's... he's only helping me. He's kind. That's all."

"Oh please. He's human. He's a man." Julian's voice has changed from disdainful to accusatory.

"What is that to mean?" Sara moves back a step, her arms still folded around her.

"They always have an ulterior motive, hidden beneath their supposed kindness, their flowery words, their grand promises. That is the nature of man. You used to understand this Sara."

"No!" She barks at him, she feels a tide of anger rising inside her, and a need to defend Joseph. "I've never believed that. They hold both the light and the dark. They can be whatever they choose to be. Joseph has no hidden motives. He has a good heart."

"Ha!" Julian laughs spitefully. "Now you are able to suddenly see into the human heart? With those mortal eyes? When you never could before?" He advances on her again, backing her up against the bedroom door. When he points a finger at her eyes, she swats his hand away.

"You DID come to torture me! Have you become so cruel? I have been punished! I am being punished, but you wish to revel in my pain and add to it."

"I am here to mitigate the damage YOU have wrought Sara!" He roars with a shocking ferocity. "The hell spawn are loosed and once more chaos will attempt to take hold in this realm. This is NOT about you!"

"Then why come to me at all?" Her own anger is boiling over as her pulse races.

"How could I not Sara? Despite everything that has transpired, you are my intended… you... were my intended."

Sara's head drops and her rage subsides. "But you are obviously free of that obligation now."

Julian starts to extend a hand to her but pulls it back just as quick. "You know you were more than an obligation to me Sara. But... you were always testing the rules. Always so reckless and headstrong."

"And it has cost me dearly. You should be happy."

"Do not play the petulant child." He snaps at her. "You may be a mortal now but you do not need to lower yourself to their level."

Sara smirks. "And that anger in your voice Julian? How very human of you."

"This is no joke Sara. You are here... consorting with this..." He points to the door and grits his teeth sharply. "You should stay far away from this mortal. That is the only warning I shall give you."

Sara glances over her shoulder at the door, thinking of Joseph such a short distance away. "Or what?" She turns back on Julian. "What are you saying? Is this a message from my Father, or are you simply speaking for yourself, for your own interests?"

"The machinations of heaven and hell are not for mortals to be privy to Sara. You will know nothing of what is to come. Do not make things worse for yourself."

"Then what am I to do?!" She gestures wildly, her patience completely spent. "Tell me!"

"That... is a mortal question." Julian states calmly, his stoic reserve returning. "The same question humans have screamed towards the heavens since the first dawning of consciousness on earth. I can give you no answers." A sadness falls over his eyes. "You are mortal Sara. I know you never fully trusted in me in the past, but you MUST learn to trust in me now." His gaze moves to the door behind her. "Farewell Sara."

A knock on the bedroom door causes Sara to turn her head. When she looks back to the room, Julian is gone. Only the fall wind remains, blowing through the open window, leaving goosebumps upon her skin.

"Sara? Is everything okay in there? You've been in there a long time." Joseph's voice comes from just the other side of the door with a tinge of worry.

She replies "Yes!" much louder and screechier than she meant to. She spots the bags of clothes on the floor where she dropped them. Regaining her calm she says, "I'm just changing. I'll be out soon."

"Okay. I'll have to leave for work soon."

"Alright Joseph. I won't be long."

"Okay."

She can hear him walk back to the living room. Sara leans against the bedroom door, absolutely refusing to let herself cry. *No! Not again!* She thinks, as she grinds her jaw from the effort of holding herself together. Sliding down to the floor, she ponders what else the fates could possibly have in store for her.

* * * * * * * * *

Chapter 5

Settling In

Sara returns to the living room several minutes later dressed in the pink Supergirl t-shirt and blue jeans. Joseph is sitting on the sofa and his jaw drops a little when he sees her. She blushes deeply from what she discovers in Joseph's eyes when he takes her in. Hunger, there is an unmistakable hunger there. While it doesn't make her uncomfortable, she does feel her body temperature rising considerably. No one in heaven or earth had ever looked at her that way.

"Do I look strange?" She twists her body around then gives him a little twirl. She does this less to try and check out her new outfit, but more to give Joseph a better look. She's loves having his eyes on her this way, making her pulse pound and her insides melt. She knows that it is only because it's Joseph watching her. If it were anyone else, mortal or angel, such a thing would be repellent, offensive. Another human contradiction she doesn't understand, but right now, she doesn't care.

"No! No, not at all. You look... really, really, good." He curses himself silently for his lack of wit and charisma. Sara smiles and bites her lip, as her blush only deepens. "I'm sorry Sara, I do need to head to work. I'll be gone for like eight or nine hours."

Her smile turns to a little pout. "Oh, Okay."

"Will you stay here please? You can watch TV and help yourself to anything in the kitchen. Really, make yourself at home."

"Can't I come with you?" She asks shyly.

"I'm sorry, I'll be working Sara. I can't really have you there for my whole shift. I mean, even I wouldn't recommend that much coffee to anyone!" He tries joking to lift her spirits.

"I've never tried coffee!" She said excitedly, hoping to change his mind.

"I'm sorry Sara... it's just not a good idea."

That was two hours ago. Sara reluctantly agreed that she would stay in the apartment until he returned home. Joseph left his cell number so he could be reached if there was an emergency. Before leaving, he turned the TV on and Sara's been flicking channels mindlessly ever since.

Almost nothing she sees makes any sense to her. It's certainly not a realistic representation of life on earth as far as she can tell. More like a contorted, funhouse mirror of the world. So much of our understanding is based on perception, she now realizes. This would seem an obvious concept, but until your perceptions are actually changed, you can't truly see it.

She pauses on a channel where a group of friends are sitting on a couch drinking from huge coffee mugs and talking. Every time one of them makes a joke, laughter emanates from out of nowhere. She finds that quite odd, but she enjoys it regardless. It makes her think of Joseph and a pang of longing hits her hard. She nearly gasps at the powerful surge of feelings within her heart.

A knock on the apartment door freezes her with fear. She holds her breath, unsure what to do. The piece of paper with Joseph's phone number rests on the coffee table. He said to call if there was an emergency. Is this an emergency?

"Sara? Dearie? It's Marjorie... Mrs. Jackson. I saw Joseph leave for work." The old woman's squeaky voice comes from the hallway. "I thought you might like some tea and sandwiches?"

Sara remembers Joseph's warning about Mrs. Jackson's interrogation skills, but she is feeling so very alone right now. "Yes! I'd like that!" She calls back and nearly falls off the sofa trying to jump to her feet. She needs a couple attempts to unlock the deadbolt before she is able to open the door.

Mrs. Jackson's smiling, bespectacled face greets her. "Hello dearie. Come on, come on." She waves for Sara to follow as she shambles back to her apartment. "We're going to have such a nice chat."

* * *

"What was with you last night?" Jill asks Joseph while he finishes washing up a herculean stack of coffee cups.

"What? Nothing." He shrugs his shoulders innocently and puts the last cup on the rack to dry.

"Oh really?" She cocks an eyebrow and puts one hand on her hip. "Does this look familiar?" In her other hand is a white apron displaying the Java Jolt logo. "I just found this in the alley out back. You told me you threw it away because it ripped."

"Hey thanks!" He takes it from her outstretched hand and she rolls her eyes and sighs.

"Be careful Joseph. You don't want to get a reputation as the weird one." She tips her head towards the door of the shop where a young woman is standing. "Customer."

He quickly ties his apron and dries his hands on it. By the time he steps up to the counter, the girl still hasn't moved. He continues to wait patiently, but she seems rooted in place, just inside the door. Her head tilts and turns oddly as she looks about the room.

He might describe her as goth, if anyone still uses that term. Maybe sixteen or seventeen years old, clad in all black. She has short, choppy blond hair and deep, dark rings around her eyes. The girl's lips are black to perfectly match her clothes. Her jeans are tattered with large holes in the knees. Her extremely white skin looks almost ghostly, bloodless. A short sleeved Sex Pistols t-shirt displays her equally pallid arms.

The odd girl continues to gawk all around her. Joseph begins to wonder what kind of drugs she might be on before her eyes come to rest on him. Finally she takes a step, then another. Her movements are atypical. It makes him think of a bad CGI character from a movie. It almost looks real to the eye, but something still feels unnatural.

The hairs on the back of his neck stand up on end and he feels an irrational sense of dread. When the girl reaches the counter, he sees the blackest eyes he's ever seen. It's as if her pupils are so dilated that they block out any color. There have only bloodshot whites surrounding black disks. Joseph plays the voice of Robert Shaw from Jaws over and over in his mind. He's saying something about a doll's eyes.

He forces a smile onto his face. "Hi there. What can I get for you?" The girl says nothing. Her disturbing eyes stare right through him. "Did you need another minute?" He tries again.

Her head tilts ever so slightly. "I've had to wait far too long already." She utters. Her voice is a cross between a child and an eighty year old chain smoker, raspy and echoing.

"I'm sorry?" He offers, while thinking, *great, a total nutcase.*

"No, you're not sorry. Not yet... Not by far. But a reckoning is coming. Be careful of which side you choose. You could be... very sorry very soon. The price of forgiveness can be high indeed." Her midnight black lips curl into a sneer.

Before a stunned Joseph can say anything else, the teenager turns away. She shuffles to the door then out onto the street. When she passes the front window, she gives him a creepy little wave before continuing on.

"What in the living hell was that?" Jill comes up behind Joseph a little too suddenly considering his anxiety level.

"I have no idea." He tries not to appear bothered. "Someone in serious need of meds I think."

"I tried to warn you. You're going to be called the weird one." She teases him.

"Hey, I was just standing here!" He fires back lightheartedly.

"Fine, fine." She rolls her eyes. "The weird magnet then."

"That's more like it! And don't think I don't notice how you always stay well away and let me handle all the problem children that come in here." This time Joseph cocks an eyebrow in semi-mock accusation.

"Hey... that's called delegating. I have complete faith in you Joseph."

They both have a laugh, but Joseph can't shake the sight of those black eyes, staring holes right through him.

* * *

"Have a seat child. Oh you are so pretty! If my boys weren't married... ha! I'd be slipping you one of their phone numbers, that's for sure." Mrs. Jackson walks Sara over to her couch. Resting on the coffee table is a platter loaded to brimming with sandwiches sliced into dainty portions. Beside the platter is a delicate China tea set, adorned with orange flowers. The floral motif is repeated around the room as well as the rest of the apartment. The couch Sara is sitting gingerly upon is upholstered with pink and red roses. The walls are covered with a fading wallpaper of butterflies, daisies and marigolds.

"Thank you very much Mrs. Jackson." She can't stop eyeing the platter of sandwiches. Hunger is such a foreign sensation for an angel, something they could never experience since they do not eat. Sara hasn't eaten since the morning and her empty stomach is making angry noises.

"Oh please, call me Marjorie. I know Joseph only thinks of me as a nosey old woman, but you and I can still be friends."

"I'm sure he doesn't think like that Marjorie."

"Oh it's okay child. I AM a nosey old woman, and he's still polite to me. I know he has trouble with people, opening up, making a connection. That's one reason I was so shocked to see him bring you home!" She leans a little closer, as if she's going to share a secret. "I'll be honest, when I saw you there, in his coat... oh well, I really didn't know what to think." Her wrinkled hand pats Sara's knee. "Now have a bite, I made those for you. There's cucumber and those ones are salmon. How do you take your tea dearie?"

Sara has no idea how she takes her tea. "Um, however you take it is fine." She picks out one of the finger sandwiches. "Have you ever tried peanut butter and Nutella?" She asks before taking a bite.

Mrs. Jackson laughs loudly. "Oh, peanut butter, yes of course, all my life. Did you know that George Washington Carver didn't actually invent it? I guess it's nice that everyone thinks he did. But it's a shame folks don't know about all the things he did do! He gave some wonderful gifts to the world, but peanut butter... as far back as the Aztecs people would grind peanuts into a paste. So it's been around a heck of a lot longer than most believe. Now Nutella I haven't tried. Me, I like my cucumber. The salmon is nice too, but only once in awhile. It can give you the heartburn you know." She sets the filled cup and saucer in front of Sara then pours her own tea.

Sara finishes her first sandwich. She's okay with the cucumber, but she liked Joseph's sandwiches a lot more. She carefully picks up the small cup by the handle and takes a sip.

"How is everything? Do you like it?"

She needs to ponder this question for a moment. The tea has both a sweet and a bitter taste to it, while she can't even figure out how to describe the taste of the sandwich. "It's delicious." She decides. "Thank you Marjorie."

"Oh it's my pleasure dear. I'm so grateful for the company." She sips her own tea while Sara samples a salmon sandwich. "When I saw Joseph go off to work and leave you here... Well, I thought you could use some company too. Especially after what happened to you." She notices the look of confusion and slight panic on Sara's face. "You getting mugged dear..."

"Yes! Yes, I was mugged." She tries to recover.

A glint appears in Mrs. Jackson's eye. "Tell me dearie, where are you from? I can hear a bit of an accent but I'll be darned if I can place it?"

The panic attacks Sara again and her mind scrambles. She doesn't want to lie, but she knows the truth is dangerous. Julian made that crystal clear. She feels the old woman's boney hand wrap around hers. She's surprised by how much strength there is in such a withered limb.

"It's alright dear. You don't need to tell me anything you don't want to. I may be old, but I can still see. I know Joseph was making up a story for my sake. If he felt he needed to do that in order to protect you, we'll that's good enough for me. I trust in that young man. He's a little lost, sure, but he'll take good care of you. That, I'm certain of. You stay by him. You stay right by his side!" There's a kindly smile on her face and meaning in her eyes.

Sara breathes a sigh of relief. "How long have you known him?" Another cucumber sandwich falls victim to Sara's ravenous appetite.

"Joseph? Oh, I guess since he moved in. That was... maybe four years ago, or is it five? It gets harder and harder to keep track of the time these days. Life can move so fast."

"Do you know him very well?" Suddenly Sara is leaning forward, literally on the edge of her seat and filled with curiosity.

"Oh, you know. I pick things up here and there. He and I don't exactly talk mind you, not like this, but I pay attention. I like to think of the people around here like my great big extended family."

Sara's eyes are bigger than the saucer her empty tea cup sits in. "Tell me about him, please Marjorie!"

Mrs. Jackson has a little laugh, saying "Now dearie, aren't YOU his friend?" then peering at Sara over her rectangular spectacles.

"Uh..."

Marjorie laughs and slaps her knee. "I'm only teasing you dearie. It's alright, you certainly don't need to be scared of me. Whatever happened to you is your business until you are ready to talk about it. I am glad you found Joseph though. I worry about him."

"Him?" The confusion returns to her eyes. "Why do you worry about him?"

"Oh well, you see, at his age, a man… or a woman too mind you, he needs to be figuring things out. He should be finding a direction, a focus, something to put himself into. Joseph has been drifting for far too long." Sara's not completely sure she understands what this means, but she listens quietly. "Now my Silas," She points to a framed photo on the credenza to her left. It's a wedding photo. In it is a young black man in a tuxedo. He's standing next to Marjorie, beautiful and radiant in her white dress. "at Joseph's age, my Silas was right where he was supposed to be... with me!" She gives Sara a sly wink and a pat on the knee, but again Sara is at a loss. "But seriously, he knew where he was going, he had a plan, and a direction. There are always going to be detours and a dead end or two, but it's all about the journey. Not standing still. That is so important in life, we all need a purpose dearie. He was such a good man, and he and I had a very good life, a blessed life."

"Silas Jackson. He passed on." Sara speaks this as if she's recalling something.

"Oh yes, ages ago, but not before we had two beautiful boys, and not before he got to hold his first grandchild. So I know he was at peace when he had to go. I truly believe that."

"Yes, he was." Sara nods knowingly. "If you can look back on your life without drowning yourself in regret, then you can truly say it was a life fulfilled."

Mrs. Jackson is taken aback. "Why... my Silas used to say just so! How about that?"

Sara looks down, a little flustered. "Yes, how about that."

"That's not to say Silas had some perfect life, mind you. He was certainly no angel when I found him. But he grew, he understood how to let go of the things he couldn't control and accept both the good and the bad. Sounds simple enough, but it's one of the toughest things a human being has to face. The fact that we're all just... human." Marjorie makes a flourish with her hands.

Sara smiles and nods. "Yes."

"Oh but you didn't want to hear about an old woman's life. You wanted to know about Joseph!" Mrs. Jackson pours herself another cup of tea. "Now remember, all I know is what I see, but when Joseph first moved in, he moved in... with a girl."

This information ties Sara's insides into a painfully tight knot. "He did?" Her eyebrows squeeze together.

Mrs. Jackson studies her reaction briefly. "Mm-hmm... a girlfriend. Very pretty, but she always seemed so cold to him. Oh, don't get me wrong, she was nice enough, but that boy was like a love starved puppy whenever I saw them together. Do you know what I mean?" She sees Sara's brows scrunching even deeper. "Some people will make others work and crawl and scrape for every little bit of affection. Doesn't necessarily mean they're bad people. It's just who they are. I think she was one of those. Then, the more distant she was with him, the more he would dote on her and fight for her attention. That kind of thing. He couldn't step back and see things for what they were. They were never meant to be together. Then, one day she was just up and gone."

"What happened?"

"Broke up. I would say that it was her that done the deed but I don't know for sure. Just my take on things. I did ask him where she was and he only told me that she moved out... but I tell you, that girl did break off a chunk of him when she left. He wasn't the same after."

"She broke his heart..."

"I should say so, or at least his spirit. That was maybe six months after they moved in, and you're the first person I've seen him with in all that time. Poor dear just goes to work then comes home. I think he must be terribly lonely." She shakes her head with a sympathetic tsk sound.

"Joseph? Really?" This doesn't seem to match with the man she met in that alley, the man she sees when she looks in his eyes. He's been so strong for her, so caring, so in charge. To imagine him alone, sad, broken... that's not the Joseph she knows.

Mrs. Jackson tilts her head and peers meaningfully at Sara. "I think he needed a push, a kick in the rear end. Something to remind him that he's still alive. Something to remind him he's still a man." She raises her eyebrows and smirks. "Or someone, hmmm. In other words... you Sara. You need to give that boy a swift kick in the behind. That's all he needs... if it's from the right person, and I think that person is you." This makes Sara blush and nearly choke on the last sandwich. "My! You certainly have an appetite don't you?! Isn't that man feeding you?" Mrs. Jackson laughs loudly at the sight of the empty platter on the table.

"I'm so sorry." Sara says, feeling utterly embarrassed.

"Oh don't be dearie. I'm only having fun. You need to laugh child!"

"Joseph makes me laugh." This thought warms her heart but also makes her miss him. "He's at work for a few more hours." She says, more to herself than Mrs. Jackson.

"You only just met him last night, didn't you? You don't need to answer. I see things. You have nowhere to go, but Joseph found you, or perhaps you were sent to him. Maybe you're meant to remind each other that you're both still alive. I am a firm believer that everything happens for a reason. It'll all unfold as it should."

Sara looks pained and shakes her head. "No. Sometimes reason is not to be found. Believe me. There is no design. If there ever was one... I don't know, but not anymore. A six year old child dying a slow painful death while her mother pointlessly prays to a God who isn't there to listen, begging for a miracle... there is no reason there. An act of mercy throwing all of existence into chaos... there is no design there. I truly wish that there was a plan, that all of this is part of a greater picture, but that picture was lost long ago. God is gone and heaven holds no sway."

"Sara! I understand it's hard to believe. We all lose faith sometimes, but believe me, I've been around such a long time, I've seen the paths that life leads us down, there is always purpose, it's we who must create our own purpose, even in the darkest of times. There is a greater picture, and every one of us paints it each day."

Sara's eyes are glistening. "I wish that were true."

Both women fall silent. The subject has brought them to a standstill.

"Maybe I should go back and wait for Joseph." She rises from the couch. "I'm sorry I got carried away. I respect your views, really I do."

The elderly woman waves the apology away with her hand. "No apologies dearie. One of the most beautiful things in this world is that we each see it with unique eyes."

"Thank you very much for the sandwiches and the tea. They were delicious."

Mrs. Jackson walks her to the door and takes her hand before she lets her leave. "Sara, there will always be darkness, as well as light. All we can do is strive to hold the light, and accept but not give in to the darkness. All paths lead somewhere, but we have to decide which turns to take."

Sara considers arguing but chooses against it. "Thank you again Marjorie. Have a nice evening."

"You too dearie. You should go and surprise that man at work. Go an' let him know he's on your mind. No man can resist that... not from such a beautiful girl as you." She gives Sara a sly wink before closing her door.

Surprise him at work..? Sara considers this as she returns to Joseph's apartment. He seemed pretty adamant that she should stay put. *I may not be an angel anymore, but I'm not a child.* She does want to see him. *Would he be happy to see me? Angry?* She feels too confined in the apartment, she's unaccustomed to such small spaces. She also feels a desire to explore the world through these mortal eyes. She had fun shopping with Joseph, she craves more experiences like that.

Java Jolt. She recalls Joseph telling her about his place of work before he went out. She bites her lower lip. Could she even find it? She has a rudimentary knowledge of the city, but not from ground level. Everything is different down here... compared to simply watching from high above.

Scanning her memory, she forms a general set of directions from the apartment to Java Jolt. She pieces most of this together from the drive to the apartment after first meeting Joseph. Once she convinces herself that she won't get lost, her thirst for adventure takes over.

Seeing the rapidly approaching sunset through the window, she digs one of Joseph's hoodies out of his closet. She did not enjoy the sensation of being cold last night. Zipping it up over her t-shirt she can't resist sniffing the sleeve.

There's a smell of paint mixed with soap. She recognises the soap smell from when she took a bath. *His soap, it smells of him...* Her desire to see Joseph intensifies considerably and her stomach does little flip-flops.

"Here I go!" She inhales deeply and with a steady hand, opens the apartment door. Her eyes wide, she steps out into the world, truly on her own, for the first time in her existence.

* * * * * * * *

Chapter 6

Part One
Julian

He returns yet again to this city. He tells himself it's only because this is where the conflagration will spark, though he knows not when nor how. He tells himself it has nothing to do with Sara, or the mortal she refuses to remove herself from. Thus he proves that angels can in fact lie, even to themselves.

For eons, long before humans trod the earth, the angels warred with demons. They battled while their Lord stood by, never interfering, never even offering a hint of guidance. It was in the midst of this madness, that the mortal realm was created. Eventually the conflict threatened to engulf the entirety of this new universe, to burn it to cinders. All the while, the souls of mankind were caught in the middle. The demons fed off the corrupted souls of mankind and grew more powerful. In time, some even become powerful enough to slay the angels.

One by one, all seven of the archangels, the Lord's first creations, were felled in battle. Their angelic forms died and their divinity rejoined with the whole. On the day the last of the seven was struck down, Julian rose to become the highest soldier of heaven. His reward from the steward of the angels for his loyalty and his ferocity. That was also the day when their Lord could no longer look away. That was the day when the most powerful representation of the divine would take on mortal form. He would shed his blood willingly and give his mortal life unto the corrupted for the sake of all humanity.

The Great Sacrifice.

By doing so, the Lord created the seals, closing off the under realm, setting the balance, and saving humanity. Only in the release of the death, could such a shift be attained. The fates always demand a balance. The seals would remain unbroken for over two thousand years… until yesterday.

In all that time, no angel was allowed to set foot nor wing in the mortal world, and that suited Julian just fine. The realms of heaven are where he wishes to be. High above. He held little if any interest in the enterprises of mankind. To him, humanity was, and is, nothing more than an experiment of his maker. An experiment which grew out of control. For if it wasn't for mortals, heaven would still be solely the domain of the angels.

Tonight Julian waits at the edge of Tache Park in the center of the urban sprawl. It is not a place many dare to enter in daylight let alone at night, unless you are looking for trouble, or know how to defend yourself. For a long time, the park has been a playground for those people on the fringes of society. A home to the homeless, a business place to those with illicit business, and a hunting ground for the souls with a taste for violence. Authorities hesitate to delve into its darkness unless they must.

The setting sun casts long shadows across the grass. They reach at Julian from the trees like slender claws. He was drawn here to this spot. Summoned. But by whom he does not know.

Noxious odours assault him and he winces, looking down his nose at their source. Three drunken men sit on a park bench not far upwind from him. One of the drunks spots Julian watching them. The man nearly does a faceplant getting up from the bench. Julian has ensured that, for the moment, no mortals can see his wings. He appears in their eyes to be as human as they. The disheveled man stumbles up the cobblestone path towards the angel.

"Hey buddy, you got any change?" The man's pants are barely staying up and his shoes have no laces. The brown stains covering his shirt and thin coat are best left a mystery.

"Have you not heard my friend? Money is the root of all evil." Julian responds haughtily.

"What?!" The man squints and furrows his brow, simultaneously almost falling over again.

"And that blessed are the poor?" Julian continues his patronizing tone. "If you DID have money, you would only purchase more poison to continue slowly killing yourself, would you not? Mouthwash... hand sanitizer... substances never meant to be ingested. For what purpose? Do you wish to die? Or are you so desperate to numb the pain of being invisible, of being less than worthless in an already worthless world that a slow death is preferable?"

Not surprisingly the man is caught completely off guard by Julian's questions. His response is exactly what Julian was expecting, anger.

"Fuck you asshole! Who the fuck... what you think?!" His slurred yelling attracts his two equally inebriated friends who have been watching from the bench. They stumble over to join their buddy threatening Julian with grievous bodily harm. None of them could follow through on the threats in their condition, not even against a normal man. Definitely not against heaven's greatest soldier.

The angel has no further interest in accommodating their insults. It only takes one fearsome look from Julian's lightning blue eyes to silence all three of the men. "Leave here." His voice rumbles like thunder. "Seek forgiveness. If you ask honestly for redemption you shall receive it. If not... then destroy yourselves far away from me mortals."

The fear of God sobers up the three lost souls and they back away without another peep. Julian watches them retreat with whatever speed their wobbly feet can muster. Then a raspy voice comes from out of the shadows.

"Suuuuch impatience. I would have expected more from such a pure representation of the divine."

Julian whirls around, his wings appear out of nowhere, spread menacingly. He faces a young woman with short blond hair and dark black eyes.

"Ardat!" There is a crash of thunder. Quick as lightning Julian reaches his right hand inside his trench coat, grasping the heavenly sword within.

"Stay your hand angel. You know I have no wish to face you in battle. Paaatience... paaatience..." She hisses.

"Even so demon, why shouldn't I cleanse you from this world as I do the blood dogs." His hand remains hidden in his coat, clutching the hilt of his sword.

Ardat laughs... actually it's more like an extra creepy slow cackle. "What for? I am no blood dog, it would do you no good to strike me down. Only a temporary measure, as you know. That was rather unfair of the creator wasn't it? To give the angels eternal life... of a sort, yet denying them an eternal soul. Was that the plan I wonder? A safeguard, once the lord realized how vulnerable-"

"You summoned me here!" Julian cuts her off. "Why?"

"Paaatience, we all know the truth angel. With the cat away, how can you not expect the mice to play. The question should be, why do you still serve a master who has forsaken you again and again. I only seek freedom, while you appear to seek subjugation."

"I seek order, while you seek chaos, nothing more. Do not attempt to color your intentions as anything else."

"Then draw your weapon angel... I will offer no resistance. You care so deeply for this mortal world? Then purge me from it, for a fortnight at least."

Ardat raises an eyebrow questioningly. Her black eyes are focused like a laser on Julian, studying him, reading him. His hand withdraws from beneath his trench coat... empty. The silvery blade of his sword is still sheathed.

"Ahhhh... so then you concede that there does exist grey in this world. That any foolish notion of black or white with no middle ground is an archaic fantasy? Or has your time sequestered away in heaven given you a new view of the eternal?" A faint smile plays over Ardat's black lips.

"I concede that dispatching you back to hell is a futile practice, but be certain Ardat, I will be watching you."

"Yes, I'm sure you will try, but while you do, don't forget to open your eyes to the rest of THIS world. This place which is neither heaven nor hell. That was it's purpose was it not? Free will? No sides unless you choose to take one? You can choose to simply turn away, not to fight. After all, you and your brethren have no real stake in what should come to pass on earth. What does it matter what happens to these inferior beings that your Lord chose to favor above his own host of angels? What does anything that happens here matter to you?" A shadow darkens her face. "Our Lord is gone."

"Enough! Put away your forked tongue and be gone demon!" Thunder rumbles again and lightning crackles in Julian's eyes.

"Very well." Ardat turns and starts to shamble away only to stop and turn back. "Of course, if it's only one mortal you are concerned about... perhaps arrangements can be made. Hmm, I'll be around. Farewell dear brother." And with that, Ardat dissolves back into the shadows, leaving Julian to rage in solitude.

He tilts his head up to the skies. "My Lord, why? WHY did you not make the path clear? Why should your angels be forced to cleanse this putrid ball of mud? Do we not deserve better?!" He bellows, knowing full well there will not be an answer. He already feels himself being pulled elsewhere. He is needed, even if it is a futile exercise. As a soldier of heaven, he will always be drawn to the dark forces whenever they threaten the innocent. With a single beat of his wings, he rises like a shot. The air rushes past him, and the clouds part like a curtain. Faster than any human eye can see, he streaks south. Another blood dog to hunt and destroy. Hell's version of cockroaches. With no seal, they can make their way to earth through any crack they can find. They come to earth to hunt, to feed on the flesh and blood of the noble hearted, the incorruptible.

As he leaves the city far behind him, he is still distracted by thoughts of Sara.

"Perhaps arrangements can be made."

Ardat's words replay in his ears no matter how hard he tries to forget them. A single word slips from Julian's lips... "Sara."

* * *

**Part Two
Sara**

Feeling equally frightened and exhilarated, Sara walks the city streets alone. She gets a funny sense of pride from successfully executing some of the utterly mundane things mortals do. Things like crossing the street when the light shows the little walking man and waiting when the red hand is flashing. Silly things yes, but somehow they make Sara feel connected to this place... they make her feel real.

So far, the buildings and streets are familiar to her. Either from walking with Joseph earlier in the day, or from the car ride the night before. She's grateful that her human memory seems to work quite well. After a thousand years of life as an angel, being suddenly human is akin to falling deaf and blind. From her perspective, to rely solely on human senses, is a monumental hurdle for her to overcome. She used to be able to see anything she wished, anywhere in the world. She could hear the beating of a fruit fly wings and the song of the whales deep in the ocean. For whatever reason, she always had trouble seeing into humans. The older angels could see all of a human's past by the merest glance into their eyes. Some of the most powerful angels could even see some of the path that lay before a mortal, if they should choose to look. But not Sara, she could only observe humans in the moment. Her mother felt that was the source of Sara's fascination with the inhabitants of earth.

As she continues down the darkening streets, most of the stores and businesses are already closed for the night. Sara peers in every window she passes. In her old life she was constantly chastised for her curiosity. It was seen as dangerous, it was not how an angel should be. She was also repeatedly warned against an excess of empathy. She was told that she must remain detached from the mortal world, that they are fleeting, while she was eternal. Now unfettered, she lets her curiosity become an unstoppable tide, sweeping her along.

Only a short while ago she told herself that she was no child, yet that is exactly how she feels. Brand new. A babe just born. A fresh spark of life, ready to grow into a flame. She can feel that fire inside of her, she craves it's heat, she craves the inferno.

A group of rowdy teenagers are making their way towards her, taking up nearly the breadth of the sidewalk. They talk and laugh loudly, swearing and shoving each other. The girls squeal and the boys bluster. Sara squeezes as close as she can to the buildings and avoids eye contact with them as they pass. She may be curious, but she's also cautious. She suddenly wishes Joseph were here to take her hand, he makes her feel so safe. She concedes that she hasn't even begun to learn how to exist in this world. The teens continue along their way without incident but she picks up her pace.

There's a corner with an old bank, with Grecian columns. I turn left there.

She refocuses on the route she planned out in her mind. She continues to walk, and walk, and walk, but she can't find the bank she's seeking. The further on she walks, the more her pulse pounds and her anxiety builds.

Oh Lord.

She can't recognize her surroundings any more. Not a single building looks familiar.

Did I go too far? Was I going the wrong way the whole time? How could I be so stupid!

She stands frozen in the middle of the sidewalk. She doesn't even know if she can find her way back to the apartment now.

If I still had my wings... She gives in to a moment of self pity before she gets a hold of herself.

No!

Gathering her wits, she takes stock of her surroundings. Down the street is an all night convenience store. The lights are shining and she sees people going in. Sara grits her teeth and heads for it.

A chime goes bing-bong as she enters the shop. It's a tiny store, but stuffed to bursting with shelves and merchandise. The guy behind the counter barely looks older than the teenagers she passed on the street. The young man is having a loud discussion with someone on his phone. He has one earbud in his ear and is holding the cord mic up near his mouth. Earbud is giving his undivided attention to the person on the other end of the phone, repeating the word "baby" pleadingly. Apparently baby is not happy. Earbud is desperately trying to convince her that he barely knows some girl named Tracy.

Making her way over to the counter, Sara waits patiently as earbud continues his conversation. She was expecting some kind of a greeting, or at least an acknowledgment that she was there. Instead, earbud ignores her completely, as if she didn't exist. He proceeds to confesses to baby that he had in fact been hanging out with Tracy on Friday night.

Sara becomes edgy. "Um..?"

"What?!" Earbud snaps at her harshly.

"I um, could you please give me directions? I think I'm lo-"

"Are you buying something?" His voice is nasty and snide.

"I don't have any money but-"

"Then get out, I'm busy." He aggressively jabs his wispy, ginger haired chin towards the door.

"Dude, she's just asking for directions, don't be such a douche."

This remark comes from a customer who has lined up behind Sara at the counter. She turns to see a man with a shaved head and more piercings in his face than most folks have on their entire body. Beside him is a heavy set woman with brown skin and shocking pink hair. A tattoo peeks out from the collar of her jacket, a rose, just below her left ear.

Sara steps aside to let them go ahead of her. The woman drops a bag of chips and a six pack of Coors on the counter. She asks the cashier for a pack of Winston's. Earbud makes a butthurt expression and starts ringing in their purchase.

"Where you trying to find?" The man with the face that mocks metal detectors asks her.

"It's a place called Java Jolt. They serve coffee. Joseph is there. I wanted to see him, surprise him at work. I was supposed to turn left at the bank with the columns but I couldn't find the bank. Now I'm kind of lost."

The man laughs. "Okay. I don't know who Joseph is, but there's a Java Jolt down on Market Avenue. Is that the one?"

Sara can only shrug.

"Well don't worry about it." The pink haired woman says as she hands her guy their bag of provisions for the night. "It's not far from where we're going, we can show you the way." She gives Sara a big friendly grin.

"Baby! Oh come on baby... Baby! You know there's nobody but you!" Earbud has already returned to pleading his case to baby.

"Thank you!" Sara's gratitude to her new saviours has left her nearly in tears. "Thank you so much!"

"Please, it's nothing." The woman replies. "I'm Tishana. This is Ivan."

"Hey!" Ivan nods a greeting.

"You new around here?" Tishana asks as the shop's door bing-bongs and they hit the streets.

Sara can't help but laugh. "VERY new! My name is Sara. You have no idea how much this means to me. Thank you again."

"Oh stop, it's nothing. Let me guess… Canadian? You're way to polite to be from here." Tishana and Ivan chuckle. Tishana digs the pack of cigarettes out of the grocery bag in Ivan's hand. The trio backtrack along the path that Sara had been wandering. Tishana lights up and takes an incredibly long drag, then opens her mouth to let the smoke slowly roll out. "Oh. My. God. I needed that."

Sara frowns. "Those are very bad for you."

Her new friend tilts her head back and expels another large cloud of smoke before speaking. "And crazy expensive too, but I'm hooked. They got me. Besides, SOMETHING'S gonna kill me, right?"

"But... but, don't you cherish your life?" Genuine confusion fills Sara's eyes. "It's such a precious thing. It's truly the greatest gift in all of existen..." She doesn't finish as a new thought forms in her head and a ponderous expression covers her face.

"Yeah, yeah, I know. We're each a special little snowflake." Tishana rolls her eyes a bit. "Sorry Sara, but I need my smokes. Just ask Ivan. Every time I try to quit, I make his life a living hell of eternal torment. Trust me."

Ivan nods comically. "Oh fuck yeah! She turns into such a raging bitch!"

Tishana hauls off and slugs his arm hard, making him yelp. "Watch it buttface!" She warns, but they both end up laughing hysterically.

Sara is fascinated by the way the two interact. "You love each other..." She mutters casually. Ivan and Tishana get a shy gleam in their eyes but they don't say anything. Sara's unexplainable need to see Joseph only grows stronger.

* * *

**Part three
Joseph**

The clock on the wall feels as if it's not only going in slow motion, but has come to a complete stop. "Is that thing moving backwards or something?" Joseph has made the same quip more than once during tonight's shift. Needless to say, he's pretty distracted. The vision of Sara's soft skin, full lips, hypnotic eyes, and silken hair won't stop dancing through his imagination. He closes his eyes and sees her before him. He surreptitiously reaches a hand out and could swear he feels his fingers playing through her dark hair. He moistens his lips and longs to taste hers upon them. This is all nothing more than a product of his vivid daydreams of course. The idea of Sara back at his apartment, awaiting his return, fills Joseph with the kind of excitement that ignites all his darkest passions.

This comes as quite a shock to him. He's had relationships in the past naturally. Three years with Denise, his last girlfriend, being the deepest. She was the first and only woman he's lived with. Joseph was firmly convinced that she was the woman he was going to grow old with. He loved her, he's sure of that, or at least he used to be sure. Otherwise the end wouldn't have been so painful, right? Otherwise he would not have been torn apart so completely, right? There are questions that continue to haunt him to this day. Most of which Joseph has tried to ignore. The biggest question being, *was ANY of it real?*

However, while he was with Denise, he gave all of his affection and attention to her. Perhaps to the point of losing himself along the way. Still, as devoted as he was to Denise, he never knew this indescribable feeling that Sara has stirred. The intense connection, the overwhelming need and desire he has for Sara, was never a part of his relationship with Denise.

He already feels all of these things and so much more for Sara. He has been trying to puzzle out what it could mean. *Is it just a surface attraction? An infatuation? Just the rush of something new?* After all, Sara is a physically stunning woman whom any heterosexual man would be attracted to on that basic level. Yet Joseph interacts with beautiful women constantly, every day, and none of them have awoken these feelings. *Is it all some damsel in distress reaction?* Joseph hasn't thought about this yet. He reminds himself that he knows nothing about Sara... except that she believes she is an angel who fell from heaven.

Who is she really? He wonders. *A victim of an assault? Some mentally or emotionally unstable person? A con artist?*

...an angel?

He shakes his head. He simply can't accept that as reality. It's not possible. His head knows that the smartest thing he could do would be to keep far, far away from her…

But he can't. His heart will not let him.

When he gives out the wrong change for the third time tonight, Jill has to comment. "You really are a million miles away today aren't you? Did that weird chick freak you out?"

Perhaps surprisingly, Joseph has all but forgotten his strange encounter from earlier. The girl with the black eyes may have unsettled him, but he brushed it off in a few minutes. He's worked in customer service jobs all his life so he's seen his fair share of odd folks. He just tells Jill "No" and shrugs it off.

"What then?" She won't let it drop. "You meet a girl or something?"

Joseph sputters noticeably and makes an embarrassed "wwwwhaaaa?" sound.

The word eureka may as well be flashing over Jill's head and her jaw drops. "Shut your mouth! No way! You have a girlfriend? When did you meet her? Is it serious? Is she hot?"

"I don't have a girlfriend!" He protests.

"Oh come on! There is definitely a woman, I can see it all over your face. Look at you! You're turning bright red! Who is she? Come on Joe, give me something!"

He's growing more embarrassed and defensive by the second. He tries his best to keep his cool and ignore her, until the bell on the front door jingles.

"JOSEPH!"

In his life, no one has uttered his name with such excitement, such joy, such longing. It makes his heart do a little slam dance in his chest. That voice... He turns to see Sara in the doorway with the biggest, most beautiful smile on her face. He feels a tidal wave of emotion crash over him.

"Sara?" His own voice is filled with confusion, astonishment, and yes... joy.

"Ooo Sara." He hears Jill tease from over his shoulder.

A bald guy with tons of piercings and a woman with pink hair are standing next to her. "So this is the famous Joseph we've heard so much about?" Ivan jokes.

With remarkable speed, Joseph is out from behind the counter and taking Sara by the hand. "Excuse us please." He says politely.

"Hey, no sweat dude. We're taking off. Just wanted to make sure Sara found you."

"Thank you so much Ivan. Thank you Tishana." She surprises them each with a full on hug. "I still hope you can quit cigarettes. I really do. This world is so much better with you in it."

The sincerity in her words surprises Tishana. "You take good care of yourself Sara. No more wrong turns okay?" She hugs her back before leaving with a wave, Ivan in tow.

Joseph nearly drags Sara by the hand to a far corner of the shop. "Sara, what are you doing here? I thought you were going to wait at home for me? Who were those people? What if you had gotten lost? What if..."

"Joseph." She frees her hand from his grasp and cups his face tenderly. "Be calm, please. Be calm." Her voice is comforting and steady. Their eyes connect deeply, forming a bridge between them. "Joseph... I needed you." Her words run through his body like an electric current, stopping and restarting his heart. "Ivan and Tishana were kind, like you. They helped me, helped me find you. I am truly sorry if I worried you or frightened you. That's the last thing I want to do, but I needed you. I can't describe it any other way."

"I just... I don't want anything to happen to you. I don't know what I'd do…"

"I know, I won't be so reckless again. I promise you Joseph." Her heart is hammering again, not out of fear, but from this incredible closeness. Her hands caress his cheeks, her sense of touch highly stimulated by the prickly hairs of his stubble beard. She wonders if Joseph is being affected the same way. His breathing is ragged and he is almost trembling under her touch.

"Thank you Sara. I... I want to keep you safe, you know? But I also know you're free to do what you want. I can't control you. I can't tell you what to do, but... if I do, when i do tell you what to do, it's only to protect you. You know that, right?" His hands find her hips of their own volition, and their bodies begin speaking to each other.

"I know that Joseph. I can feel it." Her words are breathy, strained. "I've felt it from the moment we met... I trust you Joseph."

He drops his gaze and hesitates.

"Ahem! Are you seriously not going to introduce us Joe?" Jill speaks up from the edge of the counter. Her hands are on her hips and her head is tilted to one side. Joseph rolls his eyes and Sara turns to his younger Java Jolt co-worker. Jill charges at her with a hand outstretched. "Hi there, my name is Jill. Your boyfriend here seems to have forgotten his manners, but never mind that, it's really great to meet you. Oh wow! I love those contacts! So cool! I've thought about blue ones. I hate my dull brown eyes. Ugh!"

Sara takes the outstretched hand and is given a hearty handshake as Jill rattles off her introduction. Joseph releases her hips shyly.

"I'm not her-" "He's not my-" The two speak over each other at the same time, their cheeks scarlet.

"We're not like that Jill."

"Uh-huh right Joe. Sure." She lets the sarcasm drip from her words. "You do realize the two of you were practically canoodling a second ago?"

"Canoodling?" Again they both speak over each other.

"You know what I mean." She smirks.

"Knock it off Jill." There's a stern edge in Joseph's voice that is rarely ever heard, and it makes something within Sara catch fire.

"Fine, fine. We can start closing up."

"Yeah, uh is it okay if Sara waits for me in here? I should, you know, walk her home."

Jill laughs. "Yes of course Joe. Geez I'm not going to throw out your girlfriend... I mean your *friend*." She makes finger quotes in the air.

He gives her a half-hearted thanks. Joseph despises being teased, even in good nature. He shows Sara to a table and sits her down, assuring her that he'll be finished soon. It's his turn to clean the machines, so Jill locks up then disappears behind the counter. She returns a minute later with a steaming hot cup of coffee. A mountainous dollop of whipped cream looms precariously on top of it.

"I didn't know how you liked your coffee Sara, so I made it sweet and creamy. Just a hunch." She says as she places the mug on the table in front of her. "Don't worry, it's decaf, so it won't keep you up all night." She glances over her shoulder at Joseph dismantling the espresso machine. "Unless you WANTED to stay up all night... hmmm?"

Sara can tell there's a hidden meaning to what Jill said, but she's not sure she understands it. Or else she chooses not to. These human feelings, cravings, urges, they still frighten her.

"Oh! But I don't have any money!" She exclaims, stopping herself just before taking a sip of the coffee.

"It's okay, no charge." Jill laughs and leans in close. "Girl to girl… you have to tell me, how did you two meet? I didn't think he ever goes out, let alone dates anybody! There are women in here that flirt with him all the time, but he never takes the bait. He's never even asked me out! I always figured he'd taken himself off the market." Jill laughs again. "Come on, dish!" She stares expectantly and Sara can see that she isn't going to take no for an answer.

"Well... Uh... let's just say, I needed him, and there he was!" She pauses reflectively. "He truly saved me."

"Oooo, uh oh. Sounds like you've got it bad. Haha, enjoy the coffee Sara. I need to finish cleaning up."

"Jill..?" Sara stops her before she gets away.

"Yes?"

"I think your eyes are very pretty."

"Awww… thank you Sara. Aren't you the sweetest!"

They share a smile before Jill disappears back behind the counter and Sara turns to her coffee. She sips the hot drink and savours the warmth that spreads to every part of her body. She thinks about the look of hunger she saw in Joseph's eyes earlier. She remembers the intimacy of her hands on his face. She longs for the breathless excitement that coursed through her body when Joseph put his hands on her hips. She craves the fire she felt at hearing that sharp edge in his voice.

She finds herself captured... enslaved by an overwhelming need for him,

and she likes it.

* * * * * * * *

Chapter 7

Lust

It's a little past eleven-thirty when Joseph and Sara exit the back of Java Jolt to make their way home. Sara recognizes the dingy alley where her mortal life began. She spots the dumpster that Joseph discovered her laying beside. That life changing moment. She wonders for a brief instant what would have happened to her if he hadn't seen her. She quickly decides better than to imagine what if's and instead thanked fate for bringing him to her. She has long since given up on thanking her absent Lord for anything.

With Joseph's car currently playing the role of the world's most rusted out paperweight, the pair are forced to walk home. The trip from work to his apartment takes about thirty minutes on foot. On the all too frequent occasions when his car refuses to cooperate such as this, he gladly takes the opportunity to enjoy the night air. Although, as winter approaches, the night air is becoming less and less accommodating to a leisurely stroll.

Sara stays close by his side, occasionally bumping her shoulder on his arm. They walk without saying a word to each other for quite some time. "Are you angry with me Joseph?" She finally asks.

He seems shocked by the question. "What?! No! No, I'm not angry Sara, not at all."

"Okay, but... there is something on your mind, right? I can tell." She tries to catch his eye, hoping to figure out what he's feeling. Instead Joseph stares blankly down at the sidewalk in front of them. "You don't need to tell me. I just want you to be okay."

"Sara..." He sucks in his lips then tilts his head skyward. "What's your last name?" He asks, before turning to face her.

"I... I don't have one Joseph. We don't have family names the way you do."

"You mean, angels?"

She nods, and snuffles her nose.

They cut across the street. There is virtually no traffic now and no other pedestrians are to be seen. When they reach the sidewalk on the other side, Sara grabs Joseph by the arm and brings him to a stop, face to face.

"If you don't believe me, then why are you helping me? Why do all of this for me if you think I'm some lunatic?" She doesn't try to hide the pain in her voice any more. It does hurt her, it hurts her deeply that he won't believe her.

Joseph feels a terrible stab of pain in his own heart. He dearly wants to scoop her up in his arms and tell her that he does believe her. But his head will not cease warring with his heart. Clouded by doubt and fear, his mind can't let him accept what his heart feels.

"There are... there's just so many questions Sara. That's all. I didn't mean to hurt you. I never want to hurt you."

Sara frowns but surprisingly nods in agreement. "You're right." She takes a deep breath before adding, "You're right Joseph. I'm not being fair to you. What do you want to know?"

Joseph's back straightens up like someone just gave him a wedgie. "Really!?" He blinks in astonishment.

"Yes. I mean, I shouldn't. But I guess I put you in the middle of everything the moment I accepted your help. You deserve to know... you deserve the truth, and... I trust you. So go ahead, ask anything."

There is clear resolve in her voice and Joseph can see she is one hundred percent serious. "Uh, wow! Okay." He's feeling a bit lost suddenly. "Well, uh, let's walk and talk. It's getting cold."

He gives her a tender smile that tells her everything is going to be okay. The Joseph she so desperately needed to see is back. "Yes!" She says emphatically. "I do NOT like the cold!" She wraps her arms around herself and gives a full body shiver.

Joseph realizes she's only wearing his lightweight hoodie which provides very little warmth. "Oh God, I'm sorry Sara. Here..." He puts an arm around her shoulder, snuggling her tightly to his side. Her left arm slides naturally around his waist. She already feels warmer as they resume walking.

"So... questions?" She cocks one eyebrow at him.

"Yeah... questions..." He raises his own brows, mirroring her, as well as stalling for time. "Okay, I guess there's the big one. You know, God and all that stuff. It's all real?"

"I don't know about ALL that stuff, but God was real, probably not in the way you think, but yes, God was real."

"Was real?" There's no way he wasn't going to follow up on that. "What does that mean?"

"These are very big, very long stories Joseph, but I suppose you could say that God isn't around anymore."

"What? Like God went on vacation or some-" Joseph feels Sara's body tense and she pulls up, bringing him to a halt as well. The street which had been brightly lit is inexplicably growing steadily darker. The darkness continues to spread in spite of the still shining streetlights. Joseph watches the air he exhales become a frosty vapor. The temperature surrounding the pair is plummeting at an impossible rate. Sara shivers noticeably at his side, but not merely from the cold.

"Joseph, we need to go!" She tugs at his arm. "Please, we have to go right now!"

"What's happening?"

Sara's fear is unmistakable. She tries to pull Joseph back the way they came, but the darkness has infected every avenue of escape.

"Oh Lord." She holds onto his arm so tightly that her nails dig in painfully. Suddenly she shouts at the darkness that is swallowing them. "Take me if you will, but spare him!"

"What is going on!?" He grabs Sara by the arms but all he can see in her eyes is terror. Then he hears something... a low, rumbling growl, coming from behind him.

Turning slowly, Joseph finds a hideous canine-like beast stalking towards them. The monster is huge, black as night, with a foul substance matting it's fur. Blood red eyes glow in the dark, aimed straight at him. "JESUS!" Instinctively he puts his own body between the creature and Sara.

The beast snarls loudly, charging rapidly. Claws scrape on pavement and jaws snap and snarl. Those red eyes widen, a monster from a nightmare sent here to hunt, to maim, to kill. It takes barely a second for the blood dog to cover the distance separating them. Protecting Sara any way he can is all that Joseph cares about. He leaves himself completely exposed, standing his ground in order to give her even the slightest chance of escape.

"Run!" He screams to Sara, but she refuses to leave him. Nearly upon them, the beast bears fang and claw, hungry for its blood meal.

Sara screams at an ear-splitting decibel as the blood dog leaps at Joseph.

A raspy voice in the darkness creaks loudly, "Be gone!" and in mid-jump, the blood dog is caught by the darkness itself. A massive shadow hand grabs the dog by its midsection and squeezes, crushing it until it whimpers and bursts into red flame. In an instant, the beast is reduced to nothing but black ash floating on the wind. Then the shadow hand recedes back into the surrounding darkness from whence it came.

The cloud of ash swirls past Joseph and Sara. He frantically tries to brush any of it from his person before it can settle. The unnatural darkness that had consumed the street is already receding. Joseph chokes down the lump of fear in his throat. He's still frozen in place, struggling to catch his breath and his wits. Nothing in his life makes sense anymore. Fantastical occurrences are becoming the norm, as if reality itself is tilted off its axis. *That voice...* The one that came out of the shadows, dispatching the creature. *I've heard that voice before.*

"Joseph please!" Sara is pulling on his arm again. "Let's go. Quickly! Please. Take me home."

The haze of shock lifts from his mind and he grabs Sara's hand. "Yeah, let's go!"

They move swiftly, running hand in hand, never daring to look back. They reach the apartment building in under fifteen minutes, a new record by far.

Even in the relative safety of the building, they race up the stairs to his door. Thankfully, Mrs. Jackson does not make an appearance in the hallway this night. Joseph has no idea what he would say to her. The pair are both panting hard, gasping for air. Any conversation would be virtually impossible anyway. Once the door is unlocked, they nearly tumble into the apartment and he locks the door behind them.

For a few minutes there is only the sound of two people gasping for air. Then, "O... kay... what the... hell... was that?" Joseph manages to ask between breaths.

Sara is bent over at the waist, still winded from running. "I've... never seen one... in person." She shakes her head.

"What? What is it... or was it?" He repeats.

"A blood dog." She raises her head. "A creature borne from the depths of hell itself." Joseph stares at her but says nothing. She feels tears welling in her eyes. "You still don't believe me..?"

"No Sara." He moves closer, his eyes never leaving hers. "I do believe you." Her heart makes a strange flutter. "To be honest, a part of me always did. It was just my stupid head getting in the way as usual. I do, I believe you Sara, with all my heart."

She sniffles, she's glowing, full of emotion. "And all it took was almost being eaten by a blood dog."

They both burst into boisterous, much needed laughter. The kind of laughter that hurts your sides and leaves tears streaming down your face. A safe release for the emotion and tension and fear that has weighed on their hearts.

Eventually the laughter dies away and the room falls silent. They are both breathing hard and wiping their cheeks. Joseph's eyes come to rest on Sara's chest as it rises and falls. Then he finds the exquisite lines of her slender neck. He imagines feeling her pulse against his lips as he trails kisses upon it. His gaze moves to her naturally red lips, which are parted seductively, invitingly. When her tongue runs along those same lips, leaving them moist, slick, Joseph feels his body respond. When he meets her eyes, he finds something there he didn't expect. He finds want... desire... lust. He's sure of it. He can feel it.

After Sara stopped laughing, she had to fight to catch her breath. Not in a thousand years had she laughed like that. When her eyes cleared and cheeks dried, she saw Joseph staring at her. It was more than staring. He was drinking her in, studying her, discovering her, and she loved it.

It was as if she could feel him touching her body wherever his gaze fell. He marked a trail of searing flames over her skin without laying a finger on her. An indescribable heat began to rise inside her. She exaggerated the movement of her chest, arching her back, and enjoyed his response. She reveled in the feeling of his eyes on her breasts, and imagined his hands were caressing them. She knew her cheeks must be bright red, her skin was burning hot. When his eyes came to rest on her face, she licked her lips, and she was sure she heard him make a deep growl. This time she can see much more than just hunger in his green eyes. There is a power there, an intensity, an indomitable lust. It makes her body ache and throb with expectation.

"Sara." He breathes her name like a husky demand. This is not his normal voice. Sara may not understand all that is happening to her, but she does know that this is a side of Joseph the rest of the world never gets to see.

He takes a step towards her. She makes no move, save for arching her back a little more and raising her chin. She never breaks eye contact with him, she never shies away. He is so close now, barely a sliver of space remains between them. If Joseph were to lean forward even the slightest bit, their bodies would meet. Knowing this, it is sheer agony for her to be parted from him. Yet she is unable to move. She needs him to break that last barrier, she needs him to make that one more move.

Joseph's breath is heavy and hot on her face. Without looking down, his hands find the zipper of the hoodie clinging to her body. He slowly pulls the tab down, unzipping the garment as a whimper escapes her. He slips it off her shoulders, rolling it down her arms until it comes free and lands on the floor at Sara's feet. Their lips are only a hair's breadth apart. With barely a whit of air remaining in her lungs, Sara gasps, "please."

Joseph's mouth is hard and savage on hers when he kisses her. Unrestrained at last, he is unleashed, he is free. Sara's hands grab at the belt loops of his pants to hold him as tightly to her as possible. There is no space separating them now. Their bodies crush violently against one another, trying to occupy the same space, so desperate to become one. Joseph's tongue delves deeply as they kiss recklessly, sloppily, chaotically. Sara sucks it, teasing, sparring, biting, then jamming her own tongue into his mouth in turn.

Her eyes are shut. She imagines that if she opened them she would find herself transformed into a white hot sun, a supernova. Her body no longer feels solid, it has become light, heat, energy, held together by ancient, mysterious forces. Her mind is a haze, it is aware only of the physical, the pleasure building within. She is lost in sensual immersion in the moment.

Joseph slides her t-shirt up along with her bra. When his hand squeezes her left breast brutishly, she moans into his mouth and bites down on his lower lip. She does whatever her body wishes to. He snarls at her. The tiny bud on the tip of her breast is hard beneath his palm. He slips it between his fingers, pinching and pulling on it. Sara swears for the first time, followed by the word, "yes".

He backs her up to the edge of the sofa and they topple over the arm, Joseph landing on top of her. Without a thought, Sara grabs at his coat, needing to remove anything that could keep them apart. He straddles her hips and raises himself up. He takes off the coat then yanks off his shirt. She can't take her eyes off his strong chest and flat stomach. Her mouth waters when she follows the fine line of hair leading from his chest, down his stomach, and disappearing into the waist of his pants.

She hardly notices, and wouldn't care if she did, that her soft round breasts are fully exposed. Sara WANTS Joseph to see her... She wants him to look at her with that inferno burning behind his eyes. A maelstrom of flame and fury rages out of control inside her as well, demanding her total submission. When she spots the obvious outline of Joseph's erection straining against his jeans, she feels an explosion. It is as if a dam has burst, there is a powerful heat and a throbbing wetness between her legs. "Oh... Lord." She moans.

Joseph's body is heavy on top of her again. Their insatiable mouths collide as they try to devour each other. Her fingers play in his short, wavy hair and she thrusts her tongue into his mouth assertively. Sara's hips involuntarily rise and grind her heat, her wetness, against his hardness. She can feel his excitement so explicitly. Fingers pry at the fly of her jeans. She doesn't know if they are her fingers or Joseph's but the pants come undone.

When a hand slips inside her lacy pink panties, it's definitely the firm and insistent hand of Joseph. Her back arches sharply and her body stiffens when his fingers find her most intimate spot.

"OH GOD!" She cries out.

It's at this point for Sara, that another feeling sneaks in... fear. This is all happening out of her control, even her own actions, and that is what frightens her the most.

Suddenly, the lust and intensity she saw in Joseph's green eyes changes to concern. "Are you okay Sara?" He could sense the change in her instantly. Her previous willingness, even aggressiveness, changing to hesitation and uncertainty.

He withdraws his hand from between her legs and lifts himself off of her a bit, trying to give her some space. However he also wants to remain close, to comfort her if she needs him. Basically, he doesn't know what the hell he should do.

"I'm so sorry Joseph." She tugs her t-shirt down, covering herself. She feels her nakedness now, and is torn between her feelings. She has no reason to feel ashamed, she is a human now and humans have desires, humans need sex. It is all a part of being mortal. She wonders if THAT is what truly frightened her.

"No. God no Sara, don't apologize. I'M sorry. FUCK!" Joseph precariously positions himself on his side in what little room there is on the sofa. "I got carried away. Shit! That's no excuse. I said I'd protect you. Fuck, I'm so sorry."

"Stop it Joseph." She wiggles onto her side so they are laying face to face on the sofa. "You have protected me. You've taken such good care of me." Her fingers stroke the side of his head tenderly, weaving through his hair.

"Except for jumping you just now."

"I wanted it too..." She says quietly. "But... I got scared. I've never felt feelings like this. Angels do NOT experience... this!" She gestures between them. "Physical urges." Her hand comes to rest on his bare chest, feeling his heartbeat. "Body to body, the need, the lust. That is a mortal experience, completely and totally alien to us." She catches herself. "To them."

"Should I..?" He tries to get up.

"No! Please. Can we just stay like this, lay together for a while... can you... just hold me?" She asks nervously.

"For as long as you need me." He puts an arm around her protectively and he kisses her forehead. It's a few minutes before Joseph speaks again. "Sara, what happened to you? How did you end up here?"

She nuzzles her head into his chest silently and he breathes in that smell of wildflowers in her hair. Just when he's convinced she isn't going to answer him...

"I was foolish, stupid, reckless. I let my emotions sway me and I brought disaster upon this world and all of humanity. Because of that, my Father stripped me of my divinity and banished me from heaven. I was sentenced to live a mortal life."

"Okay, but what exactly did you do that was so foolish? What was so terrible?"

Sara lets her fingers roam through his chest hair slowly. Another new experience for her. Somehow it helps calm her and she is able to put her thoughts in order. *He deserves to know.* She tells herself. "From heaven, the angels can watch over humanity, listen to their pleas. Most angels have little more than a passing interest in the toils of this world nowadays, if that. They check in on the state of things here and there, shake their heads, then turn away..."

"But you were different?"

She bobs her head in a non-committal fashion. "I guess, maybe. My parents scolded me so many times for caring too much about what was going on down here. Especially my Father. He said that earth was in the hands of the mortals now. That they needed to be responsible for their own future, that their destiny was their own, and any angel who invested themselves in the fate of humans was courting disaster. Of course i didn't listen to him. I watched and I listened and I worried. Their pains would stab at my heart and their losses would bring me to tears." She closes her eyes in contemplation, then opens them again. "There was a little girl in Iceland. Six years old, her father passed away in an accident and it was only she and her mother left behind. When we greeted her father, he implored us to watch over his wife and daughter. It's certainly not an unusual request, practically commonplace really, but I was touched by his unwavering love and devotion. So... I did watch them. The little girl, Alda, she had leukemia, and it got worse, very fast. She was so brave though, she fought so hard, finding the strength to smile for her mother no matter the pain. And her mom, she loved little Alda so much. My heart was breaking for them. As angels, we see how brief and finite mortal life is. Because of this, many angels consider a mortal life to be meaningless. But... I saw that tiny little girl, so sick and frail, but fighting so hard just to have another day with her mother and another, and another, never giving up... and I KNEW. I knew that her life was the farthest thing from meaningless." Joseph doesn't make a sound, his fingers stroke her hair, giving her comfort, lending her strength. "I broke our most sacred law. I intervened. I reached out from heaven and I took away her illness. I cured her."

"Wait!" Joseph is stunned, shaking his head in disbelief. "You saved a little girl's life, and you got kicked out of heaven for doing it? I thought that's the kind of stuff angels are supposed to do!"

"Ages ago perhaps. But Joseph, there is so much that humanity doesn't know, or has been ridiculously misunderstood. Two thousand years ago, even before I came into existence, my Lord gave the ultimate sacrifice in order to seal off hell from the mortal realm. In doing so, it was ensured that no demon or foul creature could ever walk the Earth again. The Great Sacrifice, we call it. The lord willingly gave his life to save humanity. No denizen of hell could ever again interfere in this realm. But there must always be a balance... if demons could not interfere on earth, then neither could the angels. The angels would have to willingly sequester themselves in heaven. Despite still possessing the ability, they were absolutely forbidden to interfere with events down here. To do so, would undo all that the Lord's sacrifice had accomplished. The delicate balance of this reality would tip."

"So when you saved the little girl..."

"I broke the seals of hell. I disrupted the balance. Demons can once again escape to this world. Blood dogs can find their way here, following the scent of their prey. The war between heaven and hell for the souls of humanity will begin again. All because of me." She prays that she will find compassion in Joseph's eyes, rather than judgment. She isn't disappointed.

"Oh Sara..." He kisses her lovingly on the forehead. "Whatever happens... whatever might be coming, I'll stand by you. I'm not going to let you go."

With that, Sara's walls breaks down completely. Joseph wraps her tightly in his arms. He holds her until the sobs subside. He holds her until she succumbs to exhaustion. Then he continues to hold her as a deep slumber overtakes him as well.

* * *

Standing alone in the darkened street outside Joseph's apartment building is the demon Ardat. Her black eyes are fixated on the windows above. Rain falls in frigid sheets, drenching her black clothes and white skin, but she welcomes the sensation. She has not had the opportunity to feel rain on her face since before the Great Sacrifice. Being back on earth has made it crystal clear that she has no intention of ever again returning to hell.

"Fallen angel, divine no more. Mortal... yet not mortal?" She mutters to herself. A habit formed in the dark and fetid bowels of the underworld. "What... power do you still hold? What... ARE you, little bird? And what will you become, should you return from whence you came?"

A dark shadow stretches towards the eerie young woman with the choppy blonde hair. "Questions. So many questions..." She makes a clicking sound with her tongue. "Far too many to simply leave up to the whims of fate I dare say."

She dissolves into the creeping shadow, leaving the street empty. Above, in a window on the top floor of the building she had been watching, a curtain rustles and is drawn closed. In her apartment, Mrs. Jackson slowly shuffles back to her bedroom, her expression unreadable. The old black woman stops at the edge of her bed. She grabs hold of the footboard, bracing herself, and lowers herself to her knees. Clasping her hands together, she squeezes her eyes shut and prays to heaven.

* * * * * * * *

Chapter 8

Secrets

As before, the living darkness creeps into Sara's dreams, threatening to turn them to nightmare. But something is different this time, there's a change. When the dark descends, she is not afraid, not as she was the previous night. Her heart is calm, her mind is sharp. When that voice returns, like fingernails on a chalkboard, Sara does not flinch.

"Little angel... little bird with her wings clipped... playing at being human, playing at being forgiven."

Sara squints hard into the pitch black dreamscape surrounding her. "You do not frighten me. Demon, spirit, or devil, I know you cannot hurt me here. This is not real."

"Oh it's not?" The voice asks sarcastically. "You understand dreams now? You learn so quickly? But then... is this truly a dream? Humans do not know they are dreaming while they are dreaming do they? That's the trick. So then what is... this?"

"Who are you? You who choose to hide in the shadows. I believe it is you who is afraid, not me." Sara goes on the offensive, she's sick of this game. Before becoming mortal, she was still comparatively young for an angel. She came into being well after the Great Sacrifice. Sara had never fought, never encountered any demon or beast until now. For all of her existence as an angel, hell was locked down, and she had no reason to believe it would not remain so. No training was given to her, no preparation for facing the servants of Lucifer. Whatever courage she now shows, was within her from the start.

"So... is the little bird growing a spine? Very well."

One corner of the darkness begins to warp and coalesce, taking form, becoming solid. At first, Sara is expecting another blood dog to appear and attack her. Instead, the darkness turns into a young woman, the demon Ardat. She is quite tiny and hardly strikes an intimidating figure, except for those black eyes, circled by dark rings. Eyes that bore into Sara like a drill.

"W-who are you?" She wavers a little but clings to her courage.

The young woman with the deathly pale skin smiles creepily. "You can call me Ardat, and you are correct, you have no reason to fear me."

Sara expels a high pitched, extremely sarcastic "HA!" causing Ardat to pause in surprise. "Then why did you send that blood dog after me? Why attack me in my dream last night?"

"I did NOT send the blood dog after you tonight. However, I... was the one who saved you, fallen angel. You will no doubt attract many of the dogs I'm sure. Did the angels teach you so little? No lessons on the creatures down below? I suppose they never saw the need." Ardat circles around Sara, getting lost in her own voice. "For divine beings, angels can be remarkably myopic. The blood dogs make their best meals of the good hearted. I guess it's a sort of compliment in a way if one eats you. Like... congrats on being a good person, but I'm going to eat you now." She cackles at her own joke. "And let me tell you, little bird, there are still far more terrifying creatures than the blood dogs, scratching and clawing to be freed from the underworld, believe me! As for your dream last night... let's just say, I have a flair for the dramatic."

Sara shakes her head. "And why would a demon save me from a blood dog? Why torment my dreams for that matter? I'm of no importance now, I'm just another mortal." She wishes she would wake from this dream... or whatever it is. She's sure that nothing good will come of it, and the longer it goes, the more ominous it becomes.

Ardat sighs heavily. "Why do so many feel the need to put everyone and everything into neat little categories? We always act like that's only a human trait, oh but the angels do it constantly, as do the demons. Truly, what is the difference between any of us? Do you honestly believe that every being in hell is evil? Or that every angel in heaven is good? Perhaps I saved you because I saw no reason to let you die when it was in my power to prevent it?"

"Why would you care if I live or die?"

"Why do you think God gave humans free will, but not his own angels? Punishing his most devoted servants so severely if they even questioned, and casting them out if they ever rebelled. You and I are not so different fallen angel. Perhaps, I see myself... in you."

"Were... YOU were an angel?" Sara's curiosity rises.

Ardat puts a finger to her nose, clicks her tongue and winks. "Smart little bird. No wonder you broke the boundary. You can actually think for yourself. I think... we could be extremely beneficial to each other."

A chill passes straight through Sara and she takes a step back. It feels like Ardat's voice is needling around in her head. Something isn't right.

"NO!" She states firmly.

The small, gaunt face of the demon flinches almost imperceptibly. "Hmm... too bad. Did you know... it wasn't you that the blood dog was stalking tonight. Perhaps you should think about that! It's a pity I won't be around the next time."

Sara's lavender eyes grow wide with alarm, but they are no longer looking upon Ardat. When Sara's eyes refocus, she is looking into the face of Joseph. His eyes remain closed, and his arm is draped over her. The living room is dark, it must be the middle of the night Sara guesses. A muted glow is shining through the window from the streetlights outside.

I'm awake...

She's afraid of going back to sleep, afraid of returning to that dark place. Then she notices that uncomfortable, full sensation which she now understands.

Bathroom...

Joseph looks so peaceful, she doesn't want to wake him up. Gingerly, she lifts his arm off of her midriff. He stirs a little and mumbles something about Leonard Nimoy, but continues to slumber. She tries to extricate herself from the sofa. No easy feat in her current position with her back to the coffee table. All she can do is lower herself to the floor rather than sitting up.

She's happy that she didn't disturb Joseph. He looks so cute when he's asleep, she thinks. She gets to her feet and can't resist giving him a kiss on the cheek before going to the bathroom. He smiles dreamily but doesn't wake.

Perfect. She smiles and heads to the bathroom. The fact that humans need to expel waste in this way, is the sort of thing angels choose not to think about. Sara wishes she still didn't have to, but it is what it is. She's going to have to get used to a lot of things in this life, some of them unpleasant. However, there are also some things which are proving to be immensely pleasurable.

Once she finishes with the unpleasant stuff, she considers taking a bath. When she looks in the mirror, she discovers that her bra is still pushed up above her breasts, although hidden underneath her shirt. Her tongue leisurely snakes over her lips as if searching for any lingering taste of Joseph. That was such a powerful experience. There is no other way for her to describe it. Her body temperature is already rising from thinking about it, her skin almost tingling, so she decides against the bath.

After taking off her shirt and bra, Sara dunks her head under the tap at the sink. The cool running water is refreshing and she lets her hair get drenched. There is so much on her mind right now. The passionate moment with Joseph which, although frightening, she enjoyed immensely, and then there was the dream that wasn't a dream. This is on top of just trying to get accustomed to a flesh and blood body and a new life on earth.

Ardat... Was she threatening Joseph? Was she just telling lies, playing with me? After all, that's what demons do... isn't it? But why?

She dries off her long hair as best she can with the towel. Checking the mirror again, she doesn't need to turn around to feel the scars on her back. They are the sole remnants of what she used to be. The only physical evidence that she once bore beautiful, iridescent silver wings. A constant twinge is present there, ghost sensations that never let her forget the missing part of her.

She has a sudden urge to wake Joseph up, to talk to him and hold his hand, to just BE with him. She feels like... she misses him. Which is absurd when he's just in the next room.

"What is happening to me!?" She tries to interrogate her reflection to no avail. *Are these normal human feelings?* She wonders. *How could they ever get anything accomplished? How do they even get through the day?*

She thought she understood mortal love, but that was before she became one. It seemed a simple enough thing when she was looking down from heaven. Two people meet, they feel an attraction, they get along, they fill some gap in the other, or they just need someone. That was it. Humans do not possess any divine power that would allow them to connect on a deeper level, at least that's what she used to believe. Now she's not sure what she believes.

These overwhelming feelings she is experiencing are far from simple. Angels are expected to love all equally. They do pair and bond, create offspring, but it's not exactly a matter of a romantic love. It's a matter of necessity and companionship, it's what is expected. They pair for existence, and try to make a good pairing, but love? An angel's love is a very different beast from a mortal's.

As for sex? Angels do NOT have sex.

The desire and need Sara felt when Joseph was on top of her is like nothing she could have ever imagined. *I wanted him... so badly. Sex... I wanted to have sex with him.* This thought rocks her deeply. *Is this love? Obsession? Sin? Does he feel the same? He wanted me too, that much was clear... but for what? Just for sex, or something more? Is this what Julian was warning me of?*

Sara needs to take a long, slow breath and try to push all of these ricocheting thoughts from her mind. She feels like she is going mad. Meanwhile, her body is experiencing a sense memory. The touch of Joseph's hand between her legs.

"Stop it!" She gives her head a shake.

After a very long sigh, she puts her shirt back on, sans bra. It was not very comfortable at all. Bras, yet another thing she doesn't understand the human need for. When she turns to the door, she's not sure what to do now. If she tries to lay down with Joseph again she'd surely wake him. She doesn't want that.

Opening the door and shutting off the light, she stands in the hall a moment. The bedroom door is open across from her. Unfortunately she's wide awake and has no interest in laying in bed staring at the ceiling. Her eyes move to the third door in the short hallway. It's been shut the entire time she's been here. Joseph never told her what's inside. The space it occupies is too small for a bedroom. *Storage?* She concludes.

Her curiosity has already been piqued and she opens the door. She cant see any harm in taking a peek. The smell of paint hits her instantly. It would seem that this door hasn't been opened in a very long time. The interior is dark. The bit of light from the hall allows her to make out several boxes and lots of narrow, square shapes off to one side. Cautiously peering back down the hall towards the living room, Sara doesn't see or hear any sign of Joseph.

There's a chain dangling from a fixture on the ceiling of the storage room. She gives it a yank, and with a click there is light, and it is good. She has no interest in the boxes, but the narrow shapes along the wall are another matter.

Paintings. Canvas after canvas, three rows of them lean against the wall, at least five deep.

Sara is surprised. She definitely wasn't expecting this. Joseph has never once mentioned that he is a painter or an artist. At the back of the storage room there is a color splattered easel and other supplies, but she can't take her eyes off the paintings. The nearest one depicts an old black man sitting on the steps of a run down brick and mortar building. He holds a cigarette in one hand and there is a remarkable expressiveness in his face. Sara feels as if she can see the man's entire life captured on the canvas. A difficult life, but also one filled with great reward. Incredible pain and vast love seemingly culminate in this man, in this moment, sitting on these steps.

Next to it is a painting of a pregnant woman in a soft, cream colored dress. She is standing half turned in front of a blank white backdrop. It is as though she were the only thing in existence. Her head is bowed, and her long, dark, wavy hair disguises any facial features. The woman's slender hands rest on her swollen belly wherein a new life is growing. The image is both uplifting and heartbreaking at once, and Sara is riveted by it.

The third row of paintings begins with a scene of a city street at night with a light snow falling. There is a couple sitting at a table in the window of a brightly lit restaurant. They are barely more than simple shapes but somehow they exude happiness.

Sara is overcome by the beauty in each work. Rich colors with subtle depth and composition, careful brushstrokes, and such obvious emotion and love have been put into every one. She's immersed in these worlds created by the artist.

She flips down the painting of the old man to see what's behind it. This one is a portrait of a young woman, she has deeply tanned skin and straight black hair draped over her shoulders. The brown eyes are beautiful, but distant, looking just slightly away. Despite the beauty of the subject, something feels off about it... sad.

Flipping that one down, Sara finds another featuring the same woman. This time she's in profile and her eyes are fallen. Despite the hint of a smile, it feels oddly cold to Sara. So many tiny details are recreated to perfection. The light shimmering on her silky hair. The lacy details of her sky blue colored top. The shape of her ear with her hair pulled behind it, all so exactingly rendered. It was painted with love and care, but there is a distinct gulf between subject and painter.

The next painting bears this woman once more. Sitting on Joseph's sofa, in his living room, reading a book. As with all the others, she does not look at the artist.

"Hey! What the hell do you think you're doing?"

Sara nearly jumps out of her skin. She shrieks and spins around. She was so engrossed by the paintings that she hadn't heard Joseph come up behind her. The look of anger on his face is unlike anything he has shown her in their short time together.

"Joseph! Lord, you scared me."

His expression doesn't soften. "You had NO right to snoop in here!"

"I'm-" She tries to apologize but Joseph is too angry to listen.

"This isn't your business! If I wanted you to see it, I would have shown it to you!" He's not yelling or screaming, but the trembling edge of rage in his voice, his body, his eyes, is unmistakable.

"Please Joseph..." Sara's voice is soft and pleading.

"Just go back to bed. Sleep in the bedroom." Joseph tugs the chain and turns off the light. He moves aside to let Sara out of the storage room, then closes the door.

"I'm sorry Joseph. Please..." She tries to reach a hand out to him but he storms off to the living room. So many emotions boil inside her, none of them good. Turning away, she walks into the bedroom, stunned, and closes the door quietly.

* * *

"Really, what in the world are you up to now Ardat?"

The young demon with the blond hair rolls her eyes at the tinny voice coming from nowhere. She sits on a small rise in the park, smelling the wet grass around her. The rain has ceased and most of the clouds have parted, but a damp mist remains.

"Sitting in a park, last I checked. What does it matter to you Brin?" She replies to the empty air.

A tiny puff of black smoke appears before her. It grows larger until a man, of sorts, steps from it. He stands roughly seven feet tall and is wearing a finely tailored charcoal suit. Which raises the question of who his tailor could possibly be? He has no hair, not even eyebrows, and his skin is maraschino cherry red. He has white eyes that are devoid of pupils. With each breath, the strange being billows more smoke from his mouth and nostrils.

"I'm just wondering why you're so interested in the fallen one? She's simply a mortal now. Let the blood dogs feast on her if they wish." He tilts his head to one side. "But I know you all too well." A long red finger is pointed at Ardat. "You have something in that ridiculous head of yours, don't you? Always scheming. You fall out of favor wherever you go. Even Lucifer himself dispelled you from his sight." He smirks. "So tell me, what is it? What plan is rolling about that tiny head of yours now?"

"Maybe I just enjoy playing with my prey."

"Do you think me a fool Ardat? I am no minor demon, no mindless minion, I am one of the eldest. It was I who showed you another path all those centuries ago. Do not dare to trifle with me." A crackle of flame is heard behind his words. "I want to know what you are up to."

Ardat sighs impatiently. "There is hell and there is heaven, right? And betwixt the two is earth. There are angels and there are demons, but there are also mortals. Mortals who are gifted with eternal souls, unlike angel or demon."

"We do not need immortal souls, Lucifer has gifted us with regeneration, God gave no such gift to his angels."

"Yes... if you enjoy gesssstating like a pustule within the most putrid depths of hell..." She mutters.

"And now that the seals are gone, we have nothing to fear. We will never again be trapped in our own realm." Brin gestures around him. "This world shall be our playground, and if the angels dare to oppose us, we will dispatch them as we nearly did two thousand years ago."

"And I'm sure that's enough for you." She doesn't try to hide her condescending tone.

Flame erupts from Brin's mouth and nostrils. "Watch your tongue whelp."

"Fine, fine." She lays back in the grass, letting the moisture soak into her clothes. "Turn down your furnace. It's just, yes we can come here, but then what? Is there nothing more for usss? ...I want MORE. I want to return."

"Return? Return where? Hell?"

This elicits another eye roll from Ardat. Instead of speaking, she points a finger towards the skies, towards the heavens.

Brin bursts into raucous laughter. "That's impossible! We are no longer divine, nor do we possess a mortal soul. There's no way for our kind to enter."

"Maybe..."

His blank white eyes narrow. "The fallen one? You think she can... what? Open a doorway for us? How!? That's absurd."

"Listen Brin, honestly... I don't know. All I know is that she's unique. No other has gone from being divine to being mortal... save one. Does she have an immortal soul now? Has she truly been stripped of her divinity? Can even the greatest of the angels take that from her? Has Marcellus gained so much power from the divine since the Great Sacrifice?"

Brin scoffs. "You're ridiculous. None of this matters. Just enjoy our long awaited freedom... and DON'T do anything to fuck it up for the rest us." He scowls at her and lets out a snort of flame.

Rather than offer up any more of her honest thoughts, Ardat replies, "I'm sure it will all come out to nothing. As you said, I'm being ridiculous. No need for you to concern yourself."

"Oh don't worry Ardat... I'll be keeping an eye on you."

"Feel free. The more the merrier. And by the way... I wish you would cease repeating the fiction that you somehow turned me against the angels. We both know it didn't happen that way. I made my own choices. You had nothing to do with my actions, you were only a contact. Nothing more."

Brin gives her a final snort of derision. "Whatever. I couldn't care less. Now, if you'll excuse me, there's a certain despotic madman in the east that I have been dying to whisper into the ear of.... he's absolutely NUTS!"

"Well don't go and start world War three quite yet okay? I'd kinda prefer this world wasn't reduced to ash while I'm still here."

With a hrumph and a flash of fire and brimstone, Brin disappears.

Ardat watches the clouds rolling by high above. The stars peek out then go back into hiding. Her hand runs back and forth through the grass. "Forgiveness... why do WE not deserve forgiveness? Do we not deserve the same chance for redemption as your other creations?"

A dark shadow slides over her prone form and she lets herself dissolve silently into it.

* * *

Laying in bed, Sara exerts a tremendous amount of energy to keep herself from crying.

Laying on the sofa, Joseph is plagued by regret and shame for the way he treated Sara.

Neither one can sleep, yet neither one makes a move either.

Joseph knows he overreacted. He knows Sara meant no harm. But those paintings, they hold so much pain for him. They have kept him trapped... weighed down. Ghosts, locked away in a storage room, but haunting him all the same. He has yet to find the strength to rid himself of them. They sit in the closet like Dorian Grey's portrait, never allowing Joseph to grow, never letting him move on. Out of sight, but still a constant reminder of heartbreak and loss. Now, for someone else to see them... for Sara to see them... was a debilitating humiliation. His hidden world that no one else has seen for so long, laid bare. So he snapped at her, lashed out like a child. He acted like the worst clichè of a man, when unable to deal with his feelings, he defaulted to anger. He wants to be a better man than that. But tonight, he knows he failed.

Sara knows she shouldn't have been snooping. Her innate curiosity getting her in trouble yet again. *But why did he get so mad?* Despite asking the question, she already knows the answer. The woman in the paintings. Staring at the ceiling, she tries to imagine the two of them together. She remembers Mrs. Jackson saying she made Joseph work and scrape for any sort of affection. She pictures him, attentive, doting, protective, why would anyone be cold to him?

Joseph grabs the remote from the coffee table and clicks on the TV. A Will & Grace rerun is on but he's not much in the mood to laugh. He switches to the 24 hour news to check for any stories about demonic dogs attacking people. While there are no stories in that regard, there are other suspicious items. Literally overnight, there's been a sudden and shocking rash of random or hate fuelled killings nationwide. While internationally, even the most peaceful world leaders have devolved into vitriolic rhetoric toward friend, neighbor, and enemy alike. Sara had told him there would be a war between heaven and hell for the souls of mankind. *Is this the beginning?* He wonders to himself.

Sara can hear the TV turn on in the living room. *He's still up...* She can't help but wonder if he will come to the bedroom and apologize to her.

She can't help but wonder if he will take her in his arms and hold her.

She can't help but hope that he will tell her he's sorry and everything is okay.

She can't help but dream that he will kiss her.

She watches the bedroom door for what feels like an eternity. Watching for the knob to turn. It never does, the door never opens. Eventually all hope fades, her eyelids grow heavy, and she falls into a restless, fitful sleep.

* * * * * * * * *

Chapter 9

Morning Hunger

Sara is roused by the blare of a car horn from the street outside the bedroom window. She has no clue what time it might be. Her mind is foggy and her eyes don't want to focus. There is sunlight present at the edges of the ugly, generic apartment blinds. It's just enough to make the room uncomfortably bright for her bleary eyes. She slept fully clothed on top of the covers in Joseph's bed.

Rubbing the sleep from her eyes and letting out a groan, she stretches and sits up. Taking a look down at herself, she notes that she fell asleep fully dressed. Suddenly a smell hits her like a dropped anvil. It's a wonderful smell that makes her stomach grumble and her mouth water.

Is Joseph cooking?

Her first thought of Joseph brings back all the events of the previous night... the good and the bad. She sighs and shakes her head. Dragging her weary mortal body out of bed, She strips off her clothes and takes a look at what else she has to wear.

Naturally the bedroom closet is almost completely filled by Joseph's clothes. There's a number of t-shirts and jeans of varying but subdued colors. She comes across a few dressy button up shirts and slacks too. His wardrobe could best be described as affordable and fashion safe. There's a small pile of clothes on the floor of the closet which she assumes are dirty.

Sara has one little spot in the closet where her other two t-shirts and a pair of pants hang. She makes a face. She doesn't want to put on her only clean clothes if she isn't sure what she's going to be doing today.

Laundry, they call it. Another thing I'll need to learn how to do I guess. She grumbles silently.

She decides that Joseph won't mind if she wears some of his things again. At least she hopes he won't mind. *Is he still mad at me?* She wonders. *I said sorry...*

She picks out one of his dressier button up shirts and puts it on. It's a deep burgundy with tiny white diamond designs. It has a nice sheen to it that makes her feel... well, she's not really sure how to describe it, but she likes it. The smooth fabric feels luxurious on her skin. Sara's proficiency with buttons has improved greatly since her first encounter with the infernal devices. She does up the shirt easily, leaving the top few buttons open. It hangs down to her legs and she needs to roll up the sleeves to retain proper use of her hands. Sara knows Joseph's pants won't fit her. She considers only wearing the shirt, but something tells her that might not be the best idea. So she checks out his dresser drawers for any bottoms that could fit.

Is this snooping again? She asks herself. But she finds a pair of light cotton shorts with a drawstring on the first try. *Perfect.* Once she's wearing the blue boxers she finds that with the shirt hanging down, the shorts can't be seen anyway. *Oh well.*

The intoxicating aroma coming from beyond the bedroom door continues to beckon to her. She's nervous about going out there, but she's also hungry. Besides, she can't hide in here forever. She'll have to face Joseph eventually. She didn't like him being angry with her... at least she thinks she didn't. It was such a confusing mess of feelings. It was so out of the blue and unexpected, and there was an odd excitement to it too. She comes to the conclusion that human emotions are surely going to drive her insane, then opens the door.

She hears the sound of something sizzling and nearly has to wipe the drool from her chin. Making her way into the living room, she spots Joseph at the stove with his back to her. She approaches the living room side of the breakfast bar, wary of getting too close before she knows if Joseph has calmed down. His head barely even swivels a fraction when he hears her approach. He shuts off the element before laying the last strips of sizzling bacon on a paper towel covered plate. There's a large bowl of scrambled eggs with plastic wrap over it waiting to be parceled out. On the bar sits two plates, two mugs and two glasses.

"Good morning Joseph." Sara attempts first contact. He may have mumbled something in reply, she's not sure.

What was then meant to be just a quick glance over his shoulder, turns into an almost neck breaking double take when he gets an eyeful of Sara. Her long, dark brown hair is casually tousled in a natural but extremely alluring way. Her eyes are still a little bit sleepy, as though just roused from a dream. But it's especially the sight of Sara wearing one of his shirts and seemingly nothing else that sends his pulse racing. With the top few buttons open and her shapely legs extending from beneath, it's a highly potent visual. Her bare feet shift around shyly and her toes curl, trying to conceal themselves.

Seeing Joseph eyeing her from head to toe makes Sara feel modestly confident if there is such a thing. Shy, but bold. Contradictory feelings jockey for control, and it doesn't help that she's still finding it difficult to gauge his mood. It almost feels like he's trying to hide from her. That's something he hasn't done to her before and she doesn't like it one bit.

"Do you mind if I wear some of your clothes around the apartment? I thought it would be easier if I try to keep my clothes clean..."

Her question only elicits a shrug and another mono-syllabic mumbling before he turns back to the stove. This treatment raises one emotion within Sara that she CAN understand... anger.

"Lord, Joseph, I said I was sorry okay? I know I shouldn't have been snooping... but... but..." She shouts and sputters. "Now YOU'RE being a big... big... big..."

"A big WHAT?!" Joseph's nostrils flare and his voice rises as he wheels around towards her.

"...ASSHOLE!" Sara looks downright shocked by her own choice of salty language.

"OH, I'M THE ASSHOLE!?" He explodes back at her. Leaving the empty frying pan aside, he comes around the bar to face her, pointing accusingly. "I wasn't the one digging around in someone else private stuff!"

"FOR THE LORD'S SAKE! I SAID I'M SORRY!" Sara screams in his face, practically nose to nose. Fury rages in their eyes and neither one is doing anything to hold it back. "What more do you want from me!? WHAT?!" She jabs a finger into his chest. "WHAT!?" Joseph's face turns into that of a snarling animal's. Her finger jabs at his chest again. "WHAT DO YOU WANT?!" His hands tremor.

The third time she tries to jab at him, Joseph takes hold of her wrist. His grip is firm. She can feel his strength, but it's not threatening, it's not violent. It is strong, masculine, powerful and very much in control.

The fury of their anger changes in an instant to a different sort of fire, one just as untamed and wild. With her wrist pinned inexorably in his grasp and her chest heaving, Sara grabs onto his shirt with her free hand and pulls at him. He moves in, seeking out those ruby lips, kissing her deeply. Their tongues battle passionately. His mouth, insistent and demanding, hers soft and yielding. They each find their own desperate need answered in kind. Two starving souls feeding the other.

Joseph's right hand moves to the back of her head, tangling in her silken hair, pressing her ever harder to his lips. His left hand, holding her wrist, folds her arm behind her back. He can feel Sara's nipples hard against his chest and he burns for more. When her hip rubs rhythmically against his hardness, he knows that she is burning with the same fire as he.

His lips explore her cheek, her ear, nibbling on her lobe, then kissing his way down her neck... Sara pants heavily, moaning deeply, and exhales the words, "Don't... stop."

Joseph's hands release her and for a moment she fears he's going to pull away. But before she can plead with him to continue, his fingers are grabbing clumsily at the buttons of her shirt. She bites her lip and arches her back. In his excited state he's having difficulty undoing the shirt.

She physically aches to feel his touch on her skin and Joseph is just as impatient. With a single shockingly assertive motion, he tears the shirt open, sending buttons flying everywhere. Sara gasps sharply from surprise and intense arousal. Her pupils dilate and her eyes wordlessly beg for more. Joseph's unexpected display of aggression makes her body purr, and when his mouth covers one of her hard nipples, she cries out.

"Oh GOD!"

Her hands caress his head and his tongue circles and flicks the little bud. The wetness between her legs has returned with a vengeance and she can tell that the thin shorts she's wearing are soaked through. As Joseph sucks on her nipples, his hands roam, moving to her hips, then lower. When he forcefully grabs hold of her ass, she lets out a little squeal and tosses her head back.

Her legs threaten to turn to jelly, so Joseph lowers her to the carpeted floor. He stands above her for a moment, unmistakable lust blazing in his eyes. The remnants of the burgundy shirt do not cover her gorgeous body in the least. Sara's perfect pink nipples stand rigidly at attention. Her toned stomach moves rapidly with each gasp of air. She rubs her legs together, wriggling in anticipation. Joseph can see the very obvious wet spot on the boxers she borrowed. It makes his cock strain painfully, still trapped in his jeans.

Sara watches him watching her. She doesn't know what will happen next, but she does know she will let it happen this time. Her whole body is on fire and her hands find her breasts. She runs her fingers over the nipples. They are still slippery from Joseph's tongue.

"Fuuuck."

There is truly a beast within him, Sara can see it clearly now, and she likes it. She wants him to release it, she wants his beast to take her. When he stands over her, straddling her legs, she reaches for the drawstring of her shorts. Once she has it untied, he rips them down and she kicks them off. Then, moving to kneel at her feet, Joseph spreads her legs and Sara's eyes close...

"No." He orders. "Don't close your eyes. I want to see you."

She moans, almost a growl from deep inside, and she does as he tells her, watching everything.

Her knees raised, legs bent, Joseph begins to kiss along the inside of her thighs. She's already trembling, her hips undulate, and her wetness pulses with every kiss.

Oh Lord! Sara can see such incredible focus in his green eyes, even more so than last night. She's so grateful he ordered her to keep her eyes open. His gaze burns her deliciously. She feels as if a fuse has been lit, but she's no longer afraid of the explosion… she needs it. Each time his lips touch her skin it's electric and her body responds with a jolt. She loves it. She wants more, even if she doesn't know how much more she can take. *Do mortals die of pleasure?*

His mouth moves ever closer to the throbbing heat between her legs. She's absolutely drenched, dripping onto the carpet, and it's driving him crazy. Sure, it's been a long time for Joseph, a very long time, but this is something more than just being hard up. Sara has awakened something, something no one else ever has, something that only she could.

He kisses, licks, teases, coming so very close to the spot where she needs his mouth. She tries to move into him, to meet his tongue, but his hands hold her still. She whimpers, she needs it so badly. It feels like an eternity for Sara, as Joseph tantalizes her with pleasures to be. Then, finally, his mouth falls upon her beautiful pink blossom, tasting the sweet nectar flowing forth. Sara's body turns to liquid and she squeaks something indecipherable. Her chest rises and falls violently, her fingers dig and tear into the carpet, and she would swear that she had discovered heaven on earth. Her legs reflexively try to crush Joseph's head but he forces them apart. His tongue laps at her hungrily, before lavishing attention on her prominently swollen clit.

Sara bites her lip so hard it's a miracle she doesn't draw blood. She tries to hold in a scream. Her face is a melding of desire, pleasure, and utter astonishment. Despite feeling like she's at her limit, she grabs at his head and forces him even harder into her pussy. His stubble scratches her skin harshly as he grinds his face, his mouth, his tongue, deeper into her. Their eyes never leave one another, even when her body begins to shudder and quake...

"Fuuu...!" She wails and screams like a banshee. No holding back. Her head jerks, her back arches, her hips buck, her muscles tense and spasm, and her legs quiver uncontrollably. Her breathing is high pitched and erratic. Joseph shows her no mercy, doubling his efforts. He pinches her mound between his fingers and closes his lips over her clit, sucking hard on it while his tongue plays. Her body heaves and thrashes like she's exorcising a demon and she shouts an impressive string of obscenities.

Only when her fingernails threaten to tear into his scalp does Joseph relent. His hands softly caress her still quivering legs and his wet lips kiss her thighs and knees.

Sara doesn't know if she lost consciousness, she might have even left her body. She doesn't care. All she knows right now is she has discovered pure, unadulterated ecstasy.

"Oh... my... Lord..." Is all she is capable of saying.

Her senses are hazy but she feels Joseph's arms slide under her back and her knees. The next thing she knows, she is rising up into the air. Joseph is lifting her from the floor. She links her arms around his neck and looks upon him with smouldering eyes. They say nothing as he carries her to the bedroom. She wants to drink in every feeling, every sensation. She wants to surrender to this passion, she wants to surrender to him... completely.

He lays her on his bed and she slips off the tattered remnants of his burgundy shirt, tossing it to the floor. He returns the gesture and removes his t-shirt. She takes in the sight of his lean body. As before, her gaze is drawn to the bulge in his pants and she unconsciously licks her lips.

He stands beside the bed watching her, in awe of her naked form. His cock is still painfully crammed inside his jeans and when he sees Sara lick her lips, there is no turning back. He unbuckles his belt and unzips the fly. Sara wiggles a bit in the bed, her hands intimately discovering her own body. Joseph takes his pants off, but he leaves his briefs on.

Sara swallows hard then opens her mouth, egging him on with every movement, every glance. He feels the kind of freedom and control that he's only imagined. He feels emboldened, fearless. He feels... trust.

"Sara." His voice is steady, confident. "Come here to me." He backs up several steps from the bed.

She looks surprised, but she nods. "Yes." Her lavender eyes are immense as she crawls off the bed. She comes to a stop directly in front of him and waits for his next instruction. Her cheeks, her chest are scalding. She stands completely naked before him, she is nervous, but she is also exhilarated, and more than willing to fulfill anything he desires. And so she waits.

He looks her in the eye, then tilts his head down. "Take them off." He instructs, referring to his briefs, the last bit of clothing he's wearing.

Sara's lip quivers. She can barely manage to say... "Yes." She lowers herself down to her knees. Her mouth is watering when she comes face to face, so to speak, with the straining fabric of his underwear. Slowly, deliberately, enjoying the moment, her fingers clutch at his waistband. Holding her breath, she begins to pull off his underwear, but the elastic gets caught on his erection. When she gives it a good swift tug, Joseph's cock springs free and nearly smacks her right in the face.

"Oh my god!" She laughs anxiously, but she is transfixed by it. It's not as if she's never seen the male anatomy before. After all, angels could see almost anything they wish, but this is entirely different. She finishes pulling down his briefs and Joseph steps out of them. The pulsing heat between her legs is incredible. She can't believe she could be dripping as much as she is. She can feel it, in warm rivulets running down the inside of her leg.

Joseph has a serious look on his face, almost stern. "Now... touch it."

Somehow Sara's mouth is dry and watering at the same time. "Yes." she nearly moans. Cautiously, she trails her fingers over him, starting at the base of his cock. She feels his shaft, veined and rugged, stiff, but moving as she touches it. When her fingers reach the pink and purple tip, it twitches suddenly, startling her a little. She doesn't stop though. Soon her fingers are slippery with the fluid dripping from the head of his cock.

"Take hold of it." He guides her. Joseph isn't sure where this side of him is coming from. While he wasn't passive with the other women he's been with, he did tend to hold himself back in some ways. Always hiding a part of himself from them, from everyone. But not now, not with Sara. He's enjoying this side of himself that he's never trusted enough to reveal before. "Stroke it." He orders.

This time Sara does moan as she says yes. Her hand encircles the girth of his cock and she pumps it up and down. She loves the way it makes Joseph sigh and groan, but there's too much friction. She wants it to be slippery so she can stroke it harder and faster. Out of nowhere, Sara spits onto the head of his cock and with both hands, she slathers it all over the length of his hard on.

"Oh fuck... Sara...!" Joseph groans breathlessly.

"Is that okay?" She asks, her eyes filling with concern.

"That's VERY okay." He replies and she smiles. His body sways slightly as she pumps his shaft and his breathing gets heavier. "Fuck... yes. Now... try... your mouth."

She understands his meaning, and is curious to try but she's also scared. Witnessing the effect she is already having on him helps her find her courage, empowering her. She feels free with him and she wants to experience everything. She opens her mouth...

Joseph's body shudders as Sara's tongue swirls over the head of his cock. He has to force himself to keep his eyes on her. His head keeps trying to tilt backwards against his will, but this is far too beautiful a sight to miss.

Sara is glad that he's watching her. She wants to see his face, see the lust and hunger in his eyes. She licks his length then returns to the swollen tip. She concludes that this is a highly sensitive area judging by his reactions. Her boldness increases... and she puts her lips over the large head.

"Fu... yes Sara... yes!"

She takes him all the way into her mouth. She sucks on him and sloshes her tongue around. She doesn't really know what she's doing, but it looks like Joseph is enjoying it a lot. She bobs her head up and down on his cock and drool runs down her chin. The only thing she cares about is giving him the same intense pleasure he gives her. "Show me what you like... please Joseph." She pleads when she lets him slip from her mouth.

He nods. "I will." His hands move to the back of her head and she takes him into her mouth again. His hands and hips work in concert as his cock drives into her mouth over and over. At first it's uncomfortable for her, but the demanding rawness of the act quickly arouses her in a whole new way. When he presses her head hard onto his dick, making her gag, it's more gasoline thrown onto the already raging wildfire. She sucks as hard as she can, meeting his every thrust eagerly. She hears herself snarl when Joseph's fist grabs her by the hair tightly. She takes a firm grasp of his balls in turn. Sara discovers that she too houses a beast within.

His eyes are so wild now, she loves it, she can't get enough. He pulls her off his cock by her hair and brings her to her feet. They kiss with a furious desperation. Sara's hand finds his slick member and strokes it again. Joseph's hand reaches between her legs and is immediately coated by her juices. His fingers attack her clit with impunity. She whimpers and bites at his lip until he grabs her by the shoulders roughly. Joseph pins her against the wall with a heavy slam. She smiles wantonly, making cooing sounds of excitement. His legs force hers apart and she drapes her arms around his shoulders. They are close enough that she can feel the tip of his hardness pressing against her soft wetness. Face to face, eye to eye, connected in almost every way. They both know exactly what the other wants.

One of Sara's legs rises to curl around his hip. Joseph's hands take a firm hold of her ass. They feel each other, they feel everything... and slowly, so very slowly, he presses into her. Sara's mouth gapes and she makes a high pitched sound as his hard cock penetrates her velvety pussy. She feels a profoundly beautiful pain as Joseph fills her up, inch by glorious inch.

She's incredibly tight, and Joseph groans as he pushes deeper and deeper. Her hands are clenched into fists and her breathing has lost any rhythm. When his cock is as deep inside her as it can be, he doesn't move, they remain this way, just feeling each other. Their eyes, bodies, hearts, connected... communicating in the most human, most mortal way possible.

"Oh Lord, Joseph..." She moans at last, and like that, the beast returns to his face.

Crushing her to the wall, his body starts to pound into hers. She cries out. It's a mixture of swears, screams and the word "YES!"

Both her legs lock around him, allowing his throbbing cock to delve as deeply as possible. He grunts into her ear each time his body rams into hers. She's dizzy, delirious, drowning, on fire, in heaven, in hell... and she feels the explosion building up inside her again, even greater than the first.

Joseph is fucking her hard and fast, he's not being gentle at all, he's not being tender. He's giving them both exactly what they have longed for. He needed her so badly, needed her in this way, and she needed him just as much. Covered in sweat, Sara joins Joseph thrust for thrust, slamming down onto his cock, their rhythm perfect. Her nails dig painfully into his back, which only makes him fuck her harder, savagely, unleashing his darkness.

She screams in his ear and he feels her body tense. He practically tries to ram right through her. It's a miracle that the wall doesn't give way behind her. He roars like an animal, primitive, instinctual. He feels her pussy pulsating on his cock and he pulls out at the moment they both explode as one. Clinging to one another, they ride out tremor after tremor as they are swept up in a violent, shattering orgasm.

When the strength eventually returns to Sara's wobbly legs she puts her feet to the floor. Joseph is still holding her, kissing her. This time it's softly, tenderly, lovingly. Kisses rife with meaning and emotion.

"Sara..." He's breathing hard but his eyes are warm now, completely earnest. "I... I..."

Somehow she knows exactly what he's about to say, so she kisses him to stop him from saying it. When she releases his lips, she speaks first. "I think... maybe being a mortal isn't going to be ALL bad." She smiles mischievously, and they both laugh.

Meanwhile, in the clouds high above Joseph's building, Julian hovers... watching. His wings pound against the sky like a war drum, in his eyes there is a blinding tempest of crackling lightning, and painted upon the flawless angel's face is an expression of hatred and wrath.

* * * * * * * *

Chapter 10

Oblivious

When Joseph and Sara eventually return from the bedroom, their breakfast has long since gone cold.

"Are you hungry?" He asks her.

Sara giggles at the new double meaning that question holds for her. "I am... VERY hungry." She finds that she thrills in teasing him with little innuendos. She is learning the delicate and not so delicate art of seduction. She's delighting in all of the feelings and cravings Joseph has sparked in her.

"We better eat then." His knowing smile tells her that he understood her meaning perfectly. "We need to keep our strength up." This elicits another shy giggle from Sara, and she nods in agreement.

After reheating the eggs and bacon in the microwave, Joseph divides it between them. Tucking in at the breakfast bar, they attack their plates like a pair of starving wolves. With Sara's first taste of bacon, she's found her new all-time favorite food. The sounds she makes while eating harkens back to their passionate activities of the last few hours.

The two had spent half the morning indulging in their mutual desires. The heights of their ecstasy reached and eclipsed any fantasy either could hope for. In that physical expression of intimacy, they found a closeness, a connection, neither one had expected.

Sara's body is still tingling from climaxing more times than she could count. While Joseph unleashed more than just the last four years of pent up sexual frustration. For him, it was as much about relearning how to love... as well as allowing himself the freedom to love. Forgiving himself. Letting go. He was equally rough and tender. He knew that as fragile as Sara might seem at times, she would not break at his touch. She welcomed him wholly, both his angel and his beast, without reservation, without hesitation. The bond between them only growing stronger, bound by an unbreakable thread.

When the new lovers had finally exhausted each other, Joseph held her lovingly. He kissed her again and again and gently stroked her hair. Sara felt perfectly safe and contented in that moment, she felt she had found her home. Quite remarkable, considering she had lived her entire life in heaven, for her to find that the place she belongs is in Joseph's arms.

"I really like food." She states as a matter of fact. Joseph gets a big laugh out of this, nearly spitting his orange juice. "I love it when you laugh Joseph. I also like it when you are serious... passionate... even wild. But that's different from anger isn't it? In the bedroom, you were passionate, dark, intense, but not angry... last night when I found your paintings... that was anger." Joseph is suddenly having trouble taking his eyes from his plate. "I know I was wrong for looking around but I hope you know that I didn't mean any harm? I was just looking... I want to know more about you. Can you talk to me now... can you tell me why it affected you that way?"

He nods solemnly. "I'm truly sorry I treated you that way Sara. I never told you you couldn't go in there, so I had no right to get mad the way I did... I was a gigantic asshole just like you said."

"Don't say that Joseph! I mean, thank you for apologizing, but please don't call yourself that. I was angry when I said that. I'm sorry I said it. I just wanted you to talk to me. Those paintings...? The woman..?"

He still can't look her in the eye. "It's just not easy for me to... share. You know, not that kind of thing, not with someone I... care for. It's hard for me to let anyone see my failures."

"Joseph, you are not perfect. I wouldn't want you to be perfect, I want you to be you, just imperfectly you." She rests her hand on top of his on the bar. "I want to know you, all of you. I don't want you to feel you ever need to hide any part of yourself from me. I can feel you so strongly, but I want to KNOW you too."

He laughs softly. "Tell me, are all fallen angels as amazing as you?"

She shakes her head and winks, "Nope. Just me." and they both laugh.

They continue to eat while Joseph collects his thoughts. "Okay, the paintings..." He begins falteringly. "The woman you saw in them, she was my girlfriend." Sara remains silent, letting him find his way. "We lived here together. This was a long time ago. Scary how long ago. Years ago. I met her just a little while out of high school and I guess she was my first serious... well, my only serious relationship. Oh God," he rolls his eyes, "back then I thought I was going to be some kind of world famous painter or some crazy shit like that. So stupid. But anyway, she loved my drawings and my paintings, she would light up every time I finished a new one, and I loved her... or, I don't know, I guess I thought I did. It was the deepest feeling I'd experienced at the time. She was the first woman I'd ever really let in."

The door Joseph had kept shut closed has been swung wide open. "It's funny how time changes the way you see things. I've tried so hard not to think about any of it for so long, but... I wonder, did she ever even love me, and if not, then how could I have truly loved her? Did she love the art more than the artist? She wouldn't be the person I thought she was if that was the case, right? Because I believed her, I trusted her when she said it. I would paint for her constantly. I trusted her. I spent all my free time with a brush in my hand. I'd go days without eating sometimes, I'd just be so focused on whatever piece I was in the middle of." He tilts his head and slides the last bite of eggs around his plate with the fork. "I thought things were okay between us. Maybe not amazing, maybe we didn't talk about the things we needed to talk about, and I guess I'm as much to blame for that as her. I pretended not to notice as she got more and more distant. But then, one day she just says to me she found someone else. Those were her exact words, found. Like she'd been looking. I don't know, maybe she was looking... and what did I do? I just stood there like an idiot. No idea what to do or what to say. It was like everything had collapsed around me. I was buried in the rubble, except I never died, I never got out, I was pinned down by the weight of it all. She moved out that morning, and I took down all my paintings the next day. I threw it all in the closet. I couldn't look at any of it but I couldn't get rid of it either. I couldn't paint anymore."

"You mean you stopped painting entirely? Because of her?"

"Not just because of her. I didn't have... I just couldn't anymore. I don't know. It hurt too much. I was... embarrassed, felt so stupid. I couldn't even think about picking up a brush... something inside me just turned off."

"Your heart..?"

"I don't know! I just wanted to hide everything about her. I couldn't think about it, I had to pretend it never happened. Whatever... A part of me kind of froze I think. I never wanted to let anyone in again. I never wanted to take a risk again. I never wanted to put myself out there again."

She reaches closer and grabs his arm with both hands. "Joseph! You have a gift. The way you paint, it isn't some hobby or pastime. It comes from your soul, from your heart. To deny that, to lock that away, is to deny yourself, to lock yourself away. Yes, I think you wanted to forget, but you can't forget until you let go. You did it all backwards. I may be new to human emotions, but I can see that you hid yourself in that closet. How long has it been since you let anyone in? How long has it been since you trusted someone?"

Joseph lifts his head. His deep set eyes glisten under the kitchen lights but he smiles. "I trust you Sara... you got in... and I'm so grateful for that."

He draws her in for a kiss. Her lips are soft and luxuriant. Every time they kiss, it feels like the first time, filled with mystery, passion, and portent. Her hands cup his face. There is such an intimacy when they touch, such raw emotion. She longs for him understand the depth of her feelings any way he can, whether through sight, word, or touch.

"I like kisses too." She informs him when they come up for air, licking her lips.

"Angels don't kiss?"

"Mmm... yes, they do, but it doesn't feel like this."

"See, I don't really get it. Do angels have emotions?"

"Oh of course we do. It's very different though." She crinkles her nose.

"That's extremely... vague."

"I know! I'm sorry. I don't know how to describe such a thing. As a human, I feel things with my mind, my body, my heart, and my soul, and rarely do they all feel the same thing at the same time. As an angel, I did not have a soul. I did not have a human body. Angels are a part of the divine, and with that there was always an overall sense of clarity. Even their physical form is an extension of that great power. When an angel dies, they become one with the divine from whence they came. This existence is much more chaotic. An angel's form is not a physical body in the same way a human's is. They have no physical urges, they do not need to eat or sleep. An angel feels, yes, but a mortal feels so much more. I never understood that until now... it's no wonder so many mortals falter, no wonder there is so much pain."

"But there's love too." His voice carries an emotional hitch in it that sets loose a flurry of butterflies in Sara's stomach. "But," He makes a goofy face to lighten the mood. "no angel sex huh? Didn't you mention your father? If there's no sex, then how exactly does that work?"

"Two angels bond to each other and bring a new light into the universe through the mingling of their divine essence. I am a combination of my mother and father, but not in the physical sense. I was brought to life through their divinity." She feels a heavy punch of sadness at the thought of her parents.

Only a couple of days ago, Joseph was just living his boring everyday life. Going to work, coming home, nothing exciting. Now he's discussing the inner workings of heaven and divinity over bacon and eggs with a fallen angel that he just had crazy wild sex with. Oh my, how life can change on a dime.

"What about the demons, and those big dog things, what are they going to do?"

"Create chaos I guess. Try to corrupt this world and its people, gain more power with each soul they turn." She shrugs.

"Ha!" He laughs. "I think we do a pretty good job of that on our own. No help required."

"Oh no Joseph, it will get so much worse. A dark shadow of evil will spread."

"Okay, but to what end? What can they do with the power they gain? Do demons just get a kick out of corrupting humans? Just evil for the sake of being evil, or is there a real purpose behind what they do?"

"Kind of both, I think. The eldest demons are corrupted angels of old. They sought power and rebelled. When divine power becomes corrupted, it twists the angel and they become a manifestation of the sinister shadow within them."

"God punished them."

She nods. "And banished them from heaven, but this was eons before the earth had formed, it was the infancy of the universe. So they were relegated to hell, an ancient underworld from where they could never again reach heaven."

"And when humans came along..?"

"Human souls are a unique thing, Lucifer can draw power from the corrupted souls and use it to gift his demons with regeneration and even create new demons should he wish. This is also how he retains control over his hoard. No demon dares to rise against him for fear of being eradicated with no chance for return. But regardless, the more human souls that are condemned to hell, the more powerful Lucifer and the demons become."

Joseph raises his eyebrows. "Which isn't a good thing."

"No, it's not. The angels might try to fight it. The soldiers of heaven may already be here on earth. But honestly, I don't think they can win, and I'm powerless to do anything to help." This subject is not doing anything to lighten the mood.

"I'm sorry Sara. We should talk about something else."

"No, it's okay. I just wish there was something I could do. Some way to fix what I've done. I feel so useless."

"You are not useless. Don't you dare say that Sara." She rolls her eyes at him. "Hey, come on. If you're useless, then I'm less than useless. So I do NOT want to hear that kind of self pitying bullshit talk from you ever again. Is that clear?" His stern, authoritative voice has returned, his jaw is rigid and his gaze uncompromising.

Sara nods. "Yes. I won't do that again. Thank you Joseph."

"Good." He picks up her empty plate and loads it into the dishwasher with the rest. "Now, what should we do with the rest of our day?"

"Well, the blood dogs can't come out in daylight, I know that much. You're safe outside for now... oh Lord! What about after work? Joseph, I don't want you outside after dark." She flashes back to Ardat's thinly veiled threat from her dream. "It's not safe for you."

"No worries, I'm off for two days now. I can be inside before dark."

"But what about after that?!" There's a hint of panic in her voice.

"Sara?" He squints at her. "Is there something else you're not telling me?" He fires up the dishwasher then returns to her side. He takes a hold of her by the shoulders and looks deeply into her eyes. "You know that you can tell me anything too."

"I know." She's already told him so much, and she can't in good conscience keep this from him. She recounts her dream that wasn't a dream. She tells Joseph what the demon Ardat told her about the blood dog being on the hunt for him, and her suggestion that it will happen again.

The description of the demon in Sara's dream is instantly familiar to him, he remembers the strange girl he encountered at Java Jolt. He says nothing about it though, not wanting to add to Sara's current anxiety.

"I'm scared Joseph. I can't let anything happen to you... I can't lose you."

He cloaks her in his arms. "Sara... oh baby, don't listen to anything she says. You said she's a demon, by definition they're the bad guys right? Of course she's trying to screw with your head. Don't let her get to you. We'll focus on finding a way to keep her out of your dreams, okay?"

She sniffles as she fights to control her swirling emotions. "I'm not sure if I can, but I promise I'll try."

"Good." He smiles and kisses her. "Now, shower time. I'm going to take you out this afternoon."

"Shower?" Her eyebrows arch.

"Yup."

"Mmmmm... could it be a bath instead?"

He chuckles. "Sure."

"And, could you..." she shoots him a coy look, "join me?" She asks, then bites her lip and squirms on her bar stool.

His smile transforms from warm to wicked and Sara fidgets playfully. "Yes, I think I can definitely join you." He moves closer, standing between her legs and leaning into her. She's wearing only his bathrobe, he's wearing only his briefs. Their lips hover tantalizingly close to each other. Then his hands reach beneath her to lift her off the stool. She links her arms over his shoulders as her feet lower to the floor. He kisses her passionately and she is robbed of any breath that was in her lungs. His hands work loose the tie of the robe she wears before teasing it from her shoulders. The terrycloth garment drops to the floor.

"Mmmm..." Sara feels that delicious tingle of electricity from standing naked in his sight again.

"God, you are perfect." He murmurs as he looks her over, circling her, kissing her shoulders. "Absolutely perfect." His right hand greets her bare ass with a sharp smack, making her squeal and jump. "Now get that ass in the bath. Let's get you nice and wet."

She purrs seductively and scampers to the bathroom with Joseph hot on her heels.

* * *

"ARDAT!" Julian bellows. "Show yourself! I know you are near! Your dark shadow cannot hide you dear sister, dark demon, not from me." He does nothing to hide his contempt.

The warrior angel is standing in the half finished penthouse suite of the newest Dallaire luxury hotel. Construction on the hotel had screeched to a halt months earlier when financing fell apart. The real estate mogul behind the development, Thomas Dallaire, was exposed to be little more than a cheap ponzi scheme orchestrator.

His late father had spent a lifetime building up the family name and business empire from nothing. Meanwhile, Thomas was content to coast on his father's brand and use his father's connections to make, and lose, millions of dollars many times over. Due to this lesser Dallaire, and his corrupt greed, hundreds, if not thousands, of investors lost everything they had. Retirement and pension fund managers that had expected a safe return on their group's money, were instead utterly wiped out. Dozens of contractors and businesses were left holding the bag for construction costs. Many of them were forced to go under, while others are still spending a fortune on lawsuits, seeking at least some degree of reimbursement, some measure of justice.

As for Thomas Dallaire himself? He walked away from the disaster with a tidy profit and a massive tax break. High priced lawyers and a little backroom influence were all he needed to game the system. Technically not illegal, was the term the pay for play politicians and officials parroted to the press. When one intrepid reporter managed to get a statement from the man himself, Dallaire boasted that he would run for president, saying he was the only one who could "clean up the country".

"Ardat!" Julian screams again.

"Alright, alright... don't get your feathers in a bunch. I'm right here." The pale figure of Ardat rises up out of shadows cast by sunlight streaming through the open walls of the suite. No doubt, a panoramic window view was meant for the opening. Right now it's just a big gaping hole with dislodged tarps billowing in the breeze. "Now, what are you screaming about?"

"That human, that... mortal." He snarls.

"Yeah. You'll need to be more specific angel. There's about sssevern billion of those on this ball of dirt."

"The one Sara has been..." He looks ill. "consorting with."

"Ah! Yes brother. He's not bad to look at. Don't tell me... you're jealous of a human? That would be hila-"

"Watch your tongue!" Thunder crashes when his voice rises. "I... am... not jealous."

Ardat cocks an eyebrow. "No, of course not angel. After all, you appear to be completely calm and rational right now."

"SARA..." Thunder roars again. Julian has to pause to get control of himself. He continues speaking with a semblance of calm, although through gritted teeth. "Sara... is debasing herself with that human. She is bringing shame upon herself, upon me, her parents, and the entirety of divinity. I will not allow it to continue. She is only compounding her sins. This dalliance with a human is the last straw, and it WILL end."

Ardat looks puzzled. "Her actions were entirely her own, were they not? I have looked into her eyes and unless I'm mistaken... and I know I'm not, the two of you were not yet bonded. And then there is the fact that she herself is now human! So how can anything that she might do reflect upon you in any way?"

"SHE IS MINE!" His calm shatters and lightning blazes from his eyes.

Ardat silently mouths the word *Wow*! "Okay fine, but she is a mortal now... there is nothing you can do about her little boy toy. No angel can kill a mortal without..." A light bulb clicks on. "...aaaaand that's why you're talking to me."

"You, dear sister, are a demon. You can slay the mortal for me."

"Really? You thought I would leap at the chance to kill some random human on your sssay so? Is that truly how you see your own sister? An indiscriminate killer? You believe I lust for blood and death?"

"You are my sister in name alone now Ardat. You are no angel, you are not divine, you are a foul creature of hell. So foolish you were to betray your Lord, and your betrayal was justly rewarded with damnation."

"I QUESTIONED! I SOUGHT TRUTH I SOUGHT KNOWLEDGE!" Ardat explodes.

"You consorted with a demon, you befouled yourself just as Sara is doing now."

"I dared to speak to a demon, to seek out another way, I tried to find a middle ground... and that means betrayal? I made a mistake, I trusted foolishly. I thought..." She gives up her argument. She has never once won when battling her own conscience, so she knows she will not win it now with Julian.

"You knew the price you would pay. You were a fool Ardat."

She shakes her head and sighs. "You certainly don't know much about asking others for favors do you Julian? I think perhaps your ego has finally usurped your intellect."

"Very funny, sister." He is not laughing. "Do not EVER utter my name."

"Why should I do anything to help you... brother?"

"Because, I do know you demon. I know that you will never be satisfied until you pass once more through the gates of heaven."

"So? Even if that were true, there is nothing you can do about it."

"Not now perhaps, but he who rules heaven in God's stead certainly can. The steward holds the keys as you know. He possesses the power to open or close our realm to whoever he wishes."

"Marcellus would never contradict the Lord's will, no matter how long we have been forsaken. That's why he was selected. He will ever protect the balance, even by excommunicating his own daughter. He would never restore my divinity."

"No, he would not. But Marcellus will not be steward much longer. Then I will be the next to rise. At that time, I could return to you that which you so foolishly cast aside."

Ardat eyes her brother with suspicion. "Marcellus would not sssimply step down for you."

"No. He would not." His reply is chilled with an almost reptilian cold bloodedness.

"And here I thought I was the schemer in our little family. Was that why you chose Sara to be your mate? To get closer to her father? Look for a weakness, an opening? What if he is watching you right now?"

Julian scoffs. "I learned long ago how to obscure myself from heaven's sight whenever I wish it."

"You don't care about Sara at all do you?"

"Now that is where you're wrong Ardat!" White lightning dances in his eyes. "I always intended for her to be at my side, from the first moment I saw her. She was to be mine. She still is mine, and I will not permit a filthy mortal to lay his unclean hands upon her. That is why you must kill him."

"And then what? Wait? Wait for you to assassinate Marcellus, or whatever your plan is to take his place? That's quite a stretch. Quite the leap of faith so to speak."

"I am far from being alone in desiring change in heaven. The Lord is no more. We are forsaken and have been forced to welcome an unending horde of mortal souls traipsing through our gates. I have raised more than enough support. Marcellus has refused to even listen to our reasoned arguments. It's time for action. The gates of heaven will close to those mortal souls. All those impure beings will be removed from our realm, let them wander for eternity on this rock. Heaven will once again belong to the angels alone."

Ardat laughs scornfully. "It would seem that a great deal has changed in my absence."

"Enough talk Ardat. What is your decision?" He snaps impatiently.

"I will... consider your offer."

Julian frowns and clenches his hands into fists. "Do not take long demon. My patience is finite, as is this offer."

"YOU should have a care. I have never been inclined to take orders from anyone, least of all you." Her black eyes appear to deepen and dark shapes creep around the room.

He gives her an insincere conciliatory bow. "The sooner you act... the sooner I will act Ardat. That is all."

She nods, stone faced and the shadows grow still. "I will be in touch."

A single shadow creeps up to her feet, and as if it were a pool of dark water, Ardat submerges into it.

Julian looks to the heavens. He feels dark forces tugging at him from elsewhere. More hellspawn he must hunt. He rolls his cold blue eyes. "Soon... soon this squalid realm will never concern the angels again." Stepping through the large opening in the wall, he feels sunlight cast over him. It shines and sparkles off each of the golden feathers in his wings. Outstretched, they strike a truly heavenly sight for anyone fortunate enough to catch view. He lazily rises up into the open blue sky, then accelerates off to fulfill his duty as a soldier of heaven... at least one more time.

* * *

After a lengthy and extremely steamy bath, whatever plans Sara and Joseph might have had for the rest of the day go by the wayside. Every time she would attempt to get dressed, Joseph would just end up undressing her, and vice versa. Yes, it would certainly be a day of exploration, but exploration of each other and their insatiable passion.

The bedroom, the bathroom, the kitchen, the living room, nearly every corner of the apartment became their playground. He cooked her a dinner of spaghetti with Bolognese sauce and fed it to her, sharing one plate, one fork. He would kiss sauce from her chin whenever needed and she would lick the sauce off of his lips.

When night fell, and they had physically exhausted one another, they huddled under the covers in bed. Neither of them wanted to let the day end. They kissed and talked and laughed and held on until their eyes couldn't stay open another second. It was a day that would be a perfect memory for all eternity. It was a day that would forever be a perfect moment in their lives.

Over a late breakfast the next morning they decided to take a walk to Sherritt park and have a picnic for lunch. Joseph dearly wanted to show Sara around the city a bit, but with the unreliability of his car, combined with a distinct lack of spending money, his options were limited. Sara loved the idea of a picnic anyway, all she wants is to enjoy her time with Joseph. She has seen the world for a thousand years, but now she wants to FEEL it. Through Joseph, her guide, her partner, her friend, her lover, she feels everything this world has to offer.

His heart did somersaults when he saw Sara light up at the suggestion of a picnic. So, as noon approached, Joseph prepared the ham and cheese sandwiches while Sara gathered up apples, granola bars, and drinks. They loaded all of it into a backpack, ready to head off.

Sara is dressed in her simple white polo style top and a pair of khaki beige pants. This is essentially her only other outfit. Joseph wears a faded, vintage t-shirt from a 1971 Guess Who concert, and jeans. He's a bit of an old school rock fanatic thanks to his mom who took him to a ton of concerts growing up. His favorites are The Rolling Stones and The Guess Who. The opening riff from American Woman is always his go-to ringtone.

When they get to the door, and put their shoes on, Joseph pauses. "Um, let me just grab one more thing. I'll only be a second."

"Yes, of course." Sara watches him dart to the hall at the back of the apartment. He disappears into the storage closet and there is the sound of much rummaging around. When he returns, he's carrying a sketch pad and a pencil case.

"Okay, let's go." He drops the pencil case into the backpack and slings it over his shoulder. The sketch pad gets tucked under his arm. Sara looks at him with a deeply meaningful smile and eyes filled with emotion. "Please don't make a big deal about it. It's a beautiful afternoon. I thought I might want to draw something. That's all."

She puts a hand to his cheek. "I think you're beautiful Joseph." She kisses him. A kiss that says all that needs to be said.

Joseph opens the door and as soon as his foot hits the hallway, Mrs. Jackson's door opens.

"Oh, are the two of you going out?"

"Uh, yes Mrs. Jackson. It's a nice day out." He answers politely as he locks his door.

"We're going to have a picnic in the park!" Sara blurts out excitedly, causing Joseph to groan quietly.

"Really? That sounds absolutely lovely. I haven't been on a picnic since Silas and I first started dating. That was a very long time ago, practically a different age! I know you young people don't really date anymore. You all text and facetime and hook up!" She throws her head back and laughs heartily.

"Marjorie!" Sara squeals in shocked amusement.

"I may be an old woman, but I've got cable. I keep up. I still see a whole lot with these old eyes. You'd be surprised what I know!"

Joseph is wondering how Sara knows Mrs. Jackson's first name. She's been his neighbor for six years and he didn't even know it. Regardless, his main objective right now is to extricate Sara and himself from any further conversation with his neighbor. This calls for a quick getaway.

"Marjorie! You should come with us!" Sara nearly shouts.

Joseph's eyes bulge and from the pit of his stomach he wants to scream NOOOOOOO!!! "Sara, heh, I'm sure Mrs. Jackson doesn't want to hang around with us all afternoon... and... we might do a lot of sightseeing. We don't want to walk her off her feet, right?" He nods, hoping Sara will get the message.

"Oh nonsense child. I can walk all day." Marjorie literally waves off all of Joseph's arguments. "I would LOVE to join you two."

"Great!" Sara claps.

"Great..." Joseph forces a smile. "Well then... I guess we should go."

"Let me get my shawl." Mrs. Jackson goes back into her apartment leaving Joseph alone with Sara.

"Sara!" Although his voice is hushed, the aggravation behind it is clear. "Why did you invite her along? I wanted this to be just you and me... you know?"

"Oh, I know Joseph, but she's so sweet, and I think she's lonely." She takes his hand. "Please be nice. I think you'll really like her if you give her a chance."

His eyes narrow. "Have the two of y-"

"All set!" Marjorie returns sporting a paisley shawl and Joseph's query is forced to wait for another time. She locks her door and turns to the young couple. Seeing them holding hands brings a smile to her weathered face. "I think we're going to have so much fun."

When Joseph gives a half-hearted "Mm-hm." Sara crunches his hand until he adds... "It's going to be terrific!"

She smiles and gives Joseph a kiss on the cheek. "Thank you." She whispers into his ear.

With a smile, Joseph says, "Okay then, off we go!"

Chapter 11

An Afternoon In The Park

Joseph sits in the shade of an ancient, mighty oak tree. Its leaves are yellowed and many have already fallen to the earth around him. Sherritt park is a tiny postage stamp of nature in the middle of the neighborhood. It consists of a single stone path and a handful of graffiti covered benches. Beneath him, the green grass is cool and dry. Above him, the wind rustles through the branches, creating a muted roar that brings to mind the sound of a crashing ocean surf.

He brushes a wayward leaf from the sketchpad as his pencil moves across the page. His practiced hand carefully recreates all that his eyes take in. His drawing shows Sara and Mrs. Jackson sitting on a park bench, talking, smiling, and laughing. It may not be the way he had pictured the afternoon going, but seeing Sara so happy makes his heart sing. She was right about one thing, after initially pouting and bitching about Marjorie tagging along, he did warm up to her during the walk to the park.

She gave them both an extensive history lesson of their neighborhood. She shared with them the tale of Mr. and Mrs. Nowacki, the owners of the local Polish deli. Telling of how they smuggled their new born baby out of Poland at the height of the cold war. Finding their way to this city and starting over with virtually nothing, they worked and sacrificed until they could open their own business. Now, thirty years later, they still run the deli and their daughter just opened a restaurant uptown. Joseph felt a little bit of shame for realizing he's never even been in their store.

Marjorie introduced them to a woman named Mrs. Da Costa who bumped into the group on Fort Street. She was in a terrible rush, but in a combination of English and Portuguese she told Marjorie that she had a miraculous story to tell her when she had time. She apologized, saying she was late for work and had to run.

"Prazer em conhecê-lo." Sara told her. Nice to meet you, in Portuguese. This initially took Joseph by surprise until he thought it through.

Right... angel.

Mrs. Da Costa gave them a hurried goodbye then scurried off.

"You speak Portuguese?" Mrs. Jackson asked as they continued on. Sara merely smiled and shrugged, giving a little Mm-hmm.

Marjorie was able to rattle off the history of every building they passed. There was the laundromat that was once the regional campaign office for Richard Nixon. She pointed out the karate school that used to be an x-rated video store. "Not that I ever went in there!" She added with a laugh.

Joseph couldn't help but be won over. He always wrote off Mrs. Jackson as a nosey old lady and a gossip, but now he understands that she is genuinely interested in people and their lives. The stories she passes on about his neighbors makes him feel like he knows them too.

Now, in the park, he lets the ladies have their talk while he sketches them. From an early age Joseph was extremely adept at copying subjects from life or from photographs. He could duplicate virtually any scene with remarkable aplomb. His original works however, tended to be a different story. Somehow his confidence always faltered. Nearly all of his paintings were done from photographs he took. All of them in fact, except one.

He can't hear what the two women are saying, but they are clearly having a great time. After meticulously rendering his human models, Joseph begins roughing in the trees behind them. As the whole of the picture slowly forms, he notices an odd visual. The negative space around the two women creates what looks like an aura surrounding them... almost like a halo.

"You have a gift." A scratchy voice comes from out of nowhere.

Joseph recognizes the voice even as the dark shadow of Ardat falls over his shoulder.

"She won't see me, so don't react. I'm only here to talk to you." The voice says.

Sara makes no indication that she notices anything out of the ordinary. She and Marjorie continue to talk without a care in the world. Joseph turns his head slightly to see that pale, gaunt face and dark rings encircling nearly black eyes. He remembers the choppy blonde hair and disturbing smile from their first meeting at Java Jolt.

"You?"

She makes an exaggerated look of appreciation. "Me!" Then her face turns serious. "You can call me Ardat, and I suggest you keep your eyes on the page. We don't need to worry your girlfriend, not right now at least."

He's not sure, but he decides that it's best to do what she says for now. His first thought, as always, is of keeping Sara safe. "You're a... demon?" He asks as he looks back to his drawing. Despite all he has seen, it's still difficult for him to say such things out loud without feeling crazy.

"That's right. The little lady told you all about me, did she?"

"You were in her dreams. Threatened her. You threatened me at the coffee shop too."

"Come on, threaten is such a strong word. I had to measure you. I knew you and your little fallen angel were going to be important, and here we are!"

"I'm not important, far from it." He watches Sara. She catches his eye and gives him a gorgeous smile and a wave. He waves back, trying to look casual. Mrs. Jackson looks his way too, but she is not smiling. "What do you want with me?" He speaks softly.

"Honestly? I think you are in great need of my help. So perhaps we can help each other."

Joseph's eyes are riveted to his pencil version of Sara. "I don't think I want help from a demon. Something tells me the price would be way too high."

"Heh, normally very prudent. You're not a dummy. However, in this case you definitely need help from somebody, and I don't see anyone else lining up to offer their services."

"I think we'll take our chances." He keeps his words steady and strong despite the bitter cold cast on his shoulder from Ardat's shadow.

"You won't even hear me out? Are you going to be as narrow-minded as the angels? I told you before, you would need to choose. Will you really put your trust in the ones who banished your little bird? In fact, I will not even ask you to trust me. I'm only interested in that which is mutually beneficial to both of us."

"There's nothing I can do for you." His face is like stone.

"Oh but you're wrong. The little bird will lisssten to you if you told her to help me."

"Never." He stands up and closes his sketchpad. "Nothing you say will ever convince me to help you."

Ardat frowns, her dark heart is not filled with anger, but disappointment. "Even if it were your own life which hung in the balance?"

Bending down, Joseph picks up his pencil case from the grass. As he straightens up, he stares Ardat square in the face. He doesn't need to force the strength in his voice, it comes from deep in his soul. "If I had to, I would give my life to protect Sara. Your threats don't scare me." He turns his back on the small demon and walks towards Sara and Marjorie.

"It wasn't a threa-" Ardat tries to explain, but Joseph keeps walking. "Dammit." The next moment, Ardat disappears into nothingness in the shadow of the tree.

"I want to see! Please Joseph!" Sara shouts excitedly as he approaches, holding her hands out for his sketch book.

"Alright, alright." He says with a lopsided grin. He surprises himself with his zen-like calm after essentially telling a creature of hell to go to hell. "It's nothing much, just a quick rough drawing." He immediately discounts his work but he does hand her the pad.

"Are you okay dearie?" Mrs. Jackson is watching him with concern.

He nods. "Oh yeah, I'm great." His reply and his smile do not remove the concern from her face.

"Joseph! I love this!" Sara shows his drawing to Marjorie. "Look, isn't it fantastic?"

The old woman squints at the page. "Oh my, you certainly are talented Joseph. You can truly capture a soul on the page."

He feels his cheeks reddening with embarrassment. "Thanks, really, it's nothing special. But it felt good. Felt like... ha, I don't know."

There is a bliss in Sara's heart that she has never experienced in either of her existences. She knows it is all because of Joseph. "Sit with us Joseph!" She pats the bench beside her and he snuggles up close at her shoulder.

"Now, what are the two of you planning on doing?" Marjorie asks.

"Um, I guess we'll eat." Joseph picks up the backpack at Sara's feet.

Marjorie laughs and slaps her knee. "That's good, but I meant the big picture."

"I don't understand what you mean." Sara takes the ham sandwich Joseph hands her.

He offers one to Mrs. Jackson but she shakes her head politely. "Well, you two might have been too busy to notice, but the world has gone a little crazy all of a sudden. I can see dark days ahead, and I'm sure things will get worse before they get better."

Sara is motionless with a bit of sandwich dangling out of her mouth. "Wha-what are you talking about?" She mumbles through a full mouth.

"Dearie! Manners! Never talk with food in your mouth." Joseph and Sara share confused glances as Mrs. Jackson gets back on subject. "I'm just saying, in times like these, we need to protect the ones we love. We need to open our eyes to the dangers that not only hide in the shadows, but in the light of day too. Fate will surely unfold, we can't stop that, but you need to be ready to fight and sacrifice for the people that you care about." She peers over her spectacles at them both. "Do you understand?"

Sara narrows her eyes. "Um, not really Marjorie."

Mrs. Jackson nods with a motherly look on her face. "It's okay dearie." She gives Sara a pat on the knee. "Now I should leave you young people to have some time to yourselves."

"Marjorie, you don't-"

Mrs. Jackson puts a hand up to end Sara's protestations. "It's alright child." She rises from the park bench. "It's very important for the two of you to have time alone." She turns directly to Joseph. "You are a good man, even if you haven't always seen it. Protect this girl Joseph. You know in your heart what she means to you. What the two of you have is worth protecting, it is worth nearly anything." Joseph has no response for this, he can only stare. "Now... enjoy the rest of the day you two. Bask in the sunlight while it lasts. I think it's going to be stormy tomorrow." The old woman clasps her hands in front of her chest, then turns and walks back the way they came.

"What the hell was that about? What did you say to her?"

"I don't know. She was telling me about her sons, twin boys. I guess they're both very successful... that's all."

"You didn't tell her about... you know?" His hands pantomime the flapping of wings.

"No! I didn't tell her anything. I swear!"

"Okay." He kisses her on the forehead. "I believe you Sara. I'm sorry, that was just a little disturbing considering everything that's going on."

They've both lost their appetite so they rewrap the sandwiches and tuck them into the backpack again.

"What should we do now?"

"Do you want to stop by Java Jolt on the way home?" He suggests.

"For coffee!?" Her eyes sparkle at the idea.

He laughs. "Yes, for coffee."

"Can I get whipped cream on it?"

"Anything you want kitten."

The kitten part came out of nowhere, but Sara doesn't object, in fact, it makes her feel all warm inside.

"Thank you Joseph." She smiles shyly and bites her lip.

He turns serious. "Sara, she was right about one thing. I'll always protect you, in any way I can."

She takes his hand. "I know you will, and I would do anything for you." As she steals a kiss, Joseph runs his fingers through her dark hair.

"Oh god Sara." He presses his forehead to hers. "What ARE we going to do?"

She rains tiny kisses on his lips, his cheeks, his forehead. "Whatever we do, we do it together... together!" There is so much emotion on her face, so much meaning in her voice. "I need you Joseph. I am yours, and you are mine."

"I was hoping you'd say that." He thinks for a few seconds. "Is there any way you can contact the other angels?"

She feels a bit deflated and sighs. "Prayer?"

"Do they really hear prayer?"

"Sometimes they do, if they're listening. Of course they were forbidden to act before... before I-"

"But now, if we asked for help, they might listen?"

"Joseph, I was banished, cast out in shame for breaking the most fundamental edict set by my Lord. This is all my fault. I will get no help from heaven."

She stands and turns her back, only to feel his arms around her. As ever, it makes her feel warm, safe and protected.

"To be human is to fall Sara. We fuck up all the time. Even the best of us. That's the one and only thing that's true for every single person. You said you don't want me to be perfect, well the same goes for you. I don't know what kind of standards the angels are held to, but you're a human now... and I like you just the way you are. If the angels are so self important that they won't listen to you... then I... I... I don't... really know where I was going with that... lost my train of thought."

Sara bursts out laughing and Joseph joins her.

"Let's go get that coffee." He proclaims after the laughter quiets. His arm finds its perfect home around her waist.

"With whipped cream!" She pokes him in the chest playfully.

"With whipped cream." He acquiesces.

Meanwhile, in a dark corner of a frigid Siberian forest, Julian wipes a foul, tar like residue from his gleaming silver sword. The putrid grime evaporates into smoke as he slides his fingers down the blade.

In front of him is a large puddle of the same dark slime, the only remains of a slain blood dog. Not much farther away is another puddle. Steam rises from this one like an eerie white spectre. This puddle is dark crimson in color, nearly indistinguishable from black in the moonlight. Unmoving, in the center of the pool, is the body of a teenaged boy. His throat has been torn out and his eyes are lifeless.

"It's a shame you were too late."

The scratchy voice comes from behind Julian and he pivots with the speed of lightning, his sword outstretched. The tip of the righteous blade comes to a stop only a fraction of an inch from Ardat's neck.

"It is truly unwise for a demon to sneak up on one of heaven's soldiers."

Ardat doesn't look the slightest bit impressed or intimidated. "The way I see it, I could have easily eliminated you if I had wished to angel. Don't waste your masculine posturing on me. Save it for the demons that don't know you."

He pulls back his blade and sheaths it beneath his trench coat.

"That's better." Ardat glances at the dead youth, peering into his eyes at his stolen life. "He was training for the national hockey team. He'd run these woods every morning before going to the rink no matter how cold it was. He was expecting to be drafted into the pros when he turned eighteen. Alexi, his name was Alexi."

Julian expels a disinterested sigh. "All mortals are finite on this world. Their existence is pointless. They live a few years in bags of flesh and bone then are given free providence and welcomed into heaven. Or in the case of the truly evil ones, they are tossed to Lucifer to become his playthings. It is long past time for our Lord's failed experiment to end."

"You sound like you hate them. Do you ssso despise anything that doesn't fit into your narrow image of how this universe SHOULD be?"

"You did not come here to debate the merits of lesser beings Ardat. You have made your decision?"

"I have." She replies.

"And?"

"If it means even a chance to escape this existence... I will do it. I will kill the mortal."

One corner of Julian's mouth curls. "A wise choice Ardat. Very wise."

The look of dark glee in his eyes gives her the kind of shiver she thought impossible for a demon to feel. Despite over two millennia trapped in hell, this is the first time she feels like she has made a deal with the devil. Ardat takes a long, but unnecessary breath, frosty mist slips from her lips, and mutely, she prays to the heavens for another solution.

* * *

"Sara, this is Maddy, my boss." Joseph introduces her to the heavy set woman behind the counter at Java Jolt.

"Well hello there!" Maddy has curly red hair and tons of freckles. She smiles widely at the couple, but there is obvious surprise behind the friendly expression. "Don't you get enough of this place? Now you're coming in on your day off!"

He laughs politely. "I told Sara I'd buy her a coffee."

"And whipped cream." She reminds him. Like he could ever forget. Sara grabs hold of his arm so naturally, so casually. It feels right to touch him, to hold him. Being parted from Joseph in any way feels abnormal for her, such is their indefinable yet undeniable connection.

Maddy laughs as if she was just told the funniest joke in the world, then asks, "How about a mocha with extra whipped cream? Don't worry about paying, I'll just take it out of his paycheck." She laughs hysterically again.

When Sara tries to decline, Joseph clarifies that his boss was only joking. "Oh..." She feels a little foolish for not understanding. But Joseph puts his arm around her waist and she feels better instantly. He whispers something beautiful in her ear then points her to an empty table in front of the window.

"Go sit down. I'll bring the coffee."

She is hesitant to let go of him but she does as he tells her. The chair makes a loud scraping sound when she pulls it out from the table. She watches Joseph at the counter closely. It looks like he's uncomfortable with whatever his co-workers are saying to him. He smiles along though, and they are none the wiser. Sara looks to the window at her side. Is it possible she already knows his heart so well? She watches the world outside the window. People scurrying in all directions, cars zooming by, everyone in such a rush. *Such short lives* , she thinks.

"Where are you?" Joseph asks softly as he sets a coffee cup on the table in front of her.

"I was just thinking."

Joseph settles in across from her. When she takes her first sip from the cup, the mountain of cream results in a large dollop of white foam on the end of her nose.

"You are so cute." He looks at her with such adoration. Sara uses one finger to retrieve the wayward cream from her nose. Then she runs her tongue the length of the finger, licking it clean. Joseph is helpless against the rush of passion this incites within him. He has to slide a little closer to the table to conceal his all too obvious physical reaction. "What were you thinking about just then?" He tries to keep the topic G rated.

Her eyes fall to her cup. "How long do you think we have together?"

"What do you mean Sara?"

"I've been trying so hard not to consider the reality of what I am. Don't get me wrong Joseph, you've made me so very happy, but that's sort of the point. I don't want us to end." Her emotions begin surging and she needs to remember to breathe.

He reaches out and takes her hand. "Sara, I'm not going anywhere. I'm yours and you're mine. You know that right? You can feel it, right? It's not just me."

She gasps and fights back tears. "Yes! Lord yes, I feel it!" She squeezes onto his hand as if she were dangling from a cliff. "But this life won't last. It's not fair. No matter how much I love you, there will eventually be an end, and that terrifies me. Not the idea of dying, but the idea that we will be parted in this world."

"Oh." This is definitely a bigger subject than he expected, and then something she just said hits him. "Sara... you said, you love me?"

The blush burns her cheeks and she has an urge to look anywhere except at Joseph. "I guess I did didn't I?" She controls herself and looks him in the eye. "Yes Joseph... I love you. If I know nothing else, I know that I love you. I love you."

Joseph's heart feels like it's going to burst out of his chest. "Oh God Sara, I love you too. I love you. I love you. I know it's completely crazy, but God, I love you." He can't stop saying it.

They both lean over the small table and their heads nearly collide. It's a deep, frenetic, devouring kiss, and for them it's a perfect moment. Butterflies and fireworks, fire coursing through their veins, raw primal emotion, fueled by true love.

They separate barely enough for Sara to breathe the words, "I need you Joseph. Ohhh… I need you to touch me so badly. I need to feel you inside me, oh Lord."

He also needs to catch his breath before he can reply. "Oh God yes, I need you too." Sara starts to stand up. "What about your coffee?" He asks, looking at the nearly full cup.

She doesn't take her eyes off him. A ravenous hunger burns through her. "Fuck the coffee Joseph." is all she says.

He growls under his breath and grabs her hand roughly. Pulling her with him, he murmurs in her ear, "Apartment?"

Her chest already heaving, she agrees. "Apartment."

Nearly stumbling, they walk and kiss and grope one another. Ricocheting off chairs and even the doorway, they pinball their way to the street. Everyone in the coffee shop is watching them but Joseph and Sara couldn't care less. All that matters is the entire world is the need they share and the unbridled emotions they stir in one another.

* * * * * * * * * *

Chapter 12

Eve of Darkness

Earlier in the afternoon when Sara and Joseph left Sherritt park, grey clouds were just beginning to overtake the day's blue skies. Now, as they stumble out of Java Jolt, the dark grey blanket obscures the setting sun. Still kissing, completely lost in each other, they take little notice of the approaching dark, let alone the threat of rain.

Sara recklessly walks backwards giggling, refusing to take her eyes off the man she so desires. Joseph faces her, keeping pace and reaches for her, working his right hand behind her head. His fingers are tightly tangled in her hair when he presses his mouth to hers with abandon. She forces her tongue into his mouth again, sparring with him. She loves the taste of him. It's only when the first drops of rain splash on her face that she pulls away.

"Your sketchbook!" She says with alarm.

Although he isn't nearly as concerned about his drawing as he is about feeling Sara's soft lips, Joseph quickly looks around. Spotting a nearby apartment doorstep with a stone archway entrance, he nearly picks Sara off her feet. They rush to cover, he backs her into the alcove and pins her to the wall. They are scarcely concealed from the street by a stone column. She bites her lip when she sees that look in his eye. Sara's hard nipples are testing the fabric of her damp polo shirt and her chest is rising and falling in rhythm with his. The wet shirt reveals her pink buds for any and all to see.

While Sara is partially hidden, Joseph is not. He is clearly visible to the passers-by who are rushing around trying to get out of the sudden shower. He leans into her again and kisses her hard, forcing his tongue into her mouth, demanding she give in to him. She doesn't shy away... she doesn't protest... she gives herself to him. She moans and sucks on his tongue, her hand begins rubbing his hard cock through his jeans. He lifts her shirt and roughly kneads her bare breasts. Joseph is very pleased that Sara neglected to wear her bra today. She lets out a very un-angelic swear, along with the word yes.

He can see, he can feel that she wants more. The way her body curves and grinds against his, her little whimpers that urge him to push their limits ever further. Staring deeply into her lavender eyes, he slips one hand into her pants and she gasps.

"Fuck." He grumbles when he finds her pants too constrictive. With her breasts still fully exposed, Joseph separates himself enough to use both hands to undo Sara's pants. "That's better."

"Yes... yes... touch me Joseph, please." Sara pleads eagerly.

His hand is inside her pants again, now free to give her all the pleasure he wishes. When his fingers rub her wet, tender, swollen clit, Sara nearly explodes right away. Her hands are on his shoulders, his neck, grabbing at him, clinging to him.

"You need to cum don't you Sara? Right here, right now... all those people going by. You need to cum for me don't you?" There's such an overpowering control in his voice, Sara knows she would do anything for him.

"Yes. Please. Make me cum for you. Make me cum." She squirms against him and moans, he rubs harder, faster, his fingers slippery with her lust. She trembles violently and bites down on his shoulder in an attempt to keep from screaming.

"AH, FUCK!" He grunts in pleasure and pain from her bite, feeling her throbbing heat on his fingers as her body shudders and tenses. Even with her mouth clamped onto his shoulder, she is far from quiet. It's a powerful orgasm, leaving her light headed, dizzy, and drunk.

He pulls his hand from her pants and sucks one finger clean then puts the others into her mouth. She licks them and murmurs happily. Then suddenly her eyes are wide with alarm, looking over Joseph's shoulder.

Turning, he sees a security guard in the lobby of the apartment building. He's watching them through the completely transparent glass door. The guy has the biggest grin plastered on his face. "Oh shit!" He pulls Sara's top back down as she hastily zips her pants up. Hand in hand, laughing like teenagers, the lovers make a run for it.

They race for at least a block, laughing and panting for breath, Sara's face is almost as red as her lips. Not from embarrassment, but excitement. It's not until they slow to a walk that they realize the rain showers have subsided. The city is bathed in twilight. The sun just peeks out between the clouds and the horizon, giving the streets a beautiful hue of gold. Sara is seeing so much as if for the first time. Meanwhile Joseph feels like his heart has been revived after being stilled for years.

The pair are still incapable of keeping their hands off each other. Strangers leer at them, mostly out of jealousy. Joseph has never been with someone who could stoke a fire in him this way. Particularly out in public. Heavy PDA has never been a part of any of his previous relationships. There was never the right chemistry... never the right connection.

When they come across a tiny alley, Sara gets a devilish gleam in her eye. "Your turn." She purrs. Pulling him by the hand she drags him into the alley. Not that he puts up a fight.

Disappearing behind a dumpster, Sara pushes him against a red brick wall, wet from the rain. Sliding down to her knees, ignoring the pain from the hard concrete, she stares at the outline of Joseph's cock stuffed inside his jeans. She knows it's been rigid like this since they were in Java Jolt. She undoes his belt and yanks down his zipper.

"Mmm, fuck Sara..." He groans as she tugs down his pants and briefs far enough for his cock to spring forth. The sounds of people and traffic mere feet away adds to their excitement tremendously. Two hearts thundering, two pulses racing, two passions rising uncontrollably.

Sara studies his erection for a moment, stroking it softly with her hands. Then she takes all of him into her mouth. She may be inexperienced, but she makes up for it with an intense desire. A desire to pleasure Joseph as much as he has pleasured her. She is learning him with every lick, every slurp, every stroke. She is discovering what makes him shiver, what makes him moan, what makes him growl, and what makes him cum.

Joseph is loving Sara's aggressiveness, when he feels himself building to a climax, he grabs hold of her head. Taking the lead, his hips thrust instinctively and powerfully. Sara greedily takes all that he can give her, as he fucks her mouth hard. She is exhilarated more and more every time he reveals this forceful side of himself. It drives her every bit as wild as it does him.

She sucks his cock fiercely, driven by a wanton lust. One of her hands squeezes his balls without mercy, making him flinch and groan. When she moves her hand to his ass and pushes a finger inside… Joseph erupts an epic torrent in her mouth. He lets out a very loud swear while he spurts again and again and again. His orgasm seems to last forever! Empowered, Sara thrusts her finger into his ass in rhythm with each of his spasms. She can't believe how much she loves this, or how much she craves more.

After she swallows every single drop of him, it's Joseph's turn to have wobbly legs. Sara lazily removes her finger from his ass. With cautious delicacy, she manages to tuck him back inside his pants and zip him up. Standing, she kisses him, letting him taste himself on her tongue.

His voice is raspy when he says, "Fuck... I love you Sara."

She cups his face, staring into his eyes. "I love you too Joseph. With all my heart."

Somehow they make it back to the apartment, with their lips inseparable and their passions not even remotely satiated. As soon as the door closes behind them, the sketchpad and backpack are dropped to the floor. They claw at each other's clothes like animals, tearing them off impulsively.

A moan, or a growl, or a swear, is the extent of their conversation. Moving on instinct and guided by touch, they listen to their partner's body, reacting to it. Sara's nipple is in Joseph's mouth again. He bites it, sending a jolt through her body and she tosses her head back with a tiny scream. One of his hands is gripping her ass while the other teases her other breast. She feels herself approaching the edge as his tongue lavishes her nipple, furiously sucking it, licking it, his teeth biting at it.

Her head spins as he brings her to orgasm without ever reaching between her legs. The next moment he has her in his arms, carrying her to the bedroom. Eyes locked, Sara's fingertips stroke his face, memorizing each contour. He gently lays her on the bed. Their clothing having been discarded back in the living room, both are naked and unashamed. Joseph is suspended above her, holding himself up on his arms and knees. Sara's runs her fingers through his chest hair and feels the muscles rippling beneath.

"I need to feel you inside me Joseph. I need you now. Please..." She says this with such a raw, deep honesty that his heart threatens to explode in his chest.

Her legs are spread for him, welcoming him. Sara's hand takes hold of him, never looking away from his face, and she guides him into her. They both find the same feeling when they become one... the feeling that they have found home. He rests his weight on her, kissing her lovingly, in this moment, they are a single entity. No walls, no defenses, no masks. Naked... body and soul.

She is the first to move, raising her hips to press into him and he responds. So naturally do they fall into this perfect rhythm, this most ancient dance. Face to face, eye to eye, their bodies move together. So overpowering is the emotion, that a tear falls from the corner of Sara's eye. They make love, an intimate, earth shaking, soul deep love.

His eyes speak directly to her, telling her not to hold back, to feel as deeply as she can. The tears flow freely as she surrenders, body and soul, to this engulfing love in her heart. Their bodies entwined, Sara's arms wrapped around his neck, her legs locked around his waist. She holds him so closely and he touches her so deeply. Their passion is smouldering, such tenderness and emotion, more than enough to create a heaven shattering release. They crush into each as they are both rocked by rolling swells of ecstasy.

They remain like this for what feels like eternity. Neither one is willing to let go of the moment. They hold each other, hold this feeling as long as they possibly can. Even if they know they cannot freeze time, they want this one moment to last a little longer.

Just a little longer.

* * *

Mrs. Jackson sits on her sofa watching Wheel of Fortune. Her favourite daily exercise of mental calisthenics is pitting her wits against those of the contestants. More often than not, she is successful.

"The Grapes of Wrath of Kahn!" She calls out with confidence before taking a sip of her tea.

"I'm impressed. You know Star Trek?" An eerie, scratchy voice emanates from a shadow behind the sofa.

If Marjorie is startled or confused by the voice emanating from nowhere, she disguises it marvellously. "I had two boys." She explains plainly. "Star Trek, Star Wars, X-Men, it was Mom's job to keep up with these things. Now as Nanna, it's all come back round again, funny how that always happens."

Ardat rises theatrically from the shadow with an expression of puzzlement seldom seen from a demon. "You're not afraid of me?"

Marjorie continues to watch her show. A comically hyper, grey haired woman on the TV lands on bankrupt, losing her chance at thousands of dollars and prizes. Marjorie shakes her head and offers a sympathetic tsk. "Should I be afraid of you?" She directs at the demon behind her without turning to face her.

Ardat studies the back of Marjorie's head. Heavily curled, thinning grey hair is all that is revealed. "Back at the park, I had a feeling you... saw me. You looked straight at me." She walks around the sofa and plants herself right in front of the TV, facing the old woman.

A portly, balding man in a Pittsburgh Steelers sweatshirt shouts from the TV, "The Grapes of Wrath of Kahn!" and wins the puzzle.

"But it's impossible for a mortal to sssee me unless I wish it..."

Marjorie sighs and looks Ardat in her black eyes. "I think you'll find that even on this seemingly mundane world, few things are truly impossible."

Surprise is not a sufficient word to describe Ardat's current state, she has entered complete befuddlement. "Who... who are you? I... I can't see you, into your life, your past, the way I can see others." Her eyes narrow into two thin lines, as if she were trying to stare straight through the old woman.

A small smile crosses Marjorie's face. "Oh, I'm only an old woman who has lived a very blessed life. I think all it takes to truly see things clearly is to open one's eyes, rather than shut them. Wouldn't you agree?" Marjorie takes another sip of tea then places the china cup back in its saucer on the coffee table. Her glasses are slightly misted from the steaming beverage. "Now, you have invited yourself into my home. I think good manners dictate that you introduce yourself." The mist on her glasses dissipates.

It takes something truly shocking to leave a demon speechless, but Ardat is left searching for words. "Uh... well. My... Uh name is Ardat."

Mrs. Jackson nods. "Thank you Ardat. My name is Marjorie. Why don't you tell me, where do you come from Ardat?"

The demon manages to collect herself and thinks before speaking. "Somehow... I think you already know exactly where I come from. I just don't know how you could know."

Marjorie nods again, looking like the cat that swallowed the canary, and offers the demon a seat beside her. "I think dearie... that we need to have a talk."

* * *

Sara stirs, her head is resting on Joseph's chest, his arm beneath her. Their naked bodies are warm, tangled together under the blankets. She can't actually recall falling asleep, but she's not surprised. She feels so comfortable, so safe with Joseph. Everything is so natural, everything fits. At peace in his arms. No nightmares. Protected. Completely at home with his heart sounding like thunder in her ear, booming, powerful, hypnotic, a force of nature.

Her peace is suddenly shattered by terror when she senses another presence in the darkened room. A shadowed figure stands stoically in the corner near the door. There is only the faint glow of the moon shining through the window. Immediately she moves to wake Joseph.

"Do not bother." The dark silhouette directs her.

Squinting down at the man she has given her newly mortal heart to, Sara finds him in an unnaturally deep sleep. Ignoring what the intruder told her, she shakes his shoulders and calls his name to no avail, he continues to slumber undisturbed.

"I told you. He will not wake until I allow it."

"Stop this Julian!" She screams. "Leave him alone! Leave us alone."

Taking one step into the pale beam of moonlight, the blonde angel in the long black trench coat comes into view. His skin looks ghostly white while his electric blue eyes are hidden in darkness, creating a ghoulish vision.

A trick of the light. Sara thinks.

"I am giving you only one last chance Sara. Leave here now. Never return. Never see this mortal again. I am showing you kindness with this warning Sara. I will not show you such kindness again."

Sara is used to hearing cold detachment in his voice, but this is new. Now there is a dark malevolence. "And if I don't..?" The tremor in her voice is impossible to hide no matter how hard she tries to mask it.

Although his shadowed eyes are hidden from her, Sara is certain he is watching Joseph, asleep in her arms.

"Then I will not be responsible for the consequences. I could have saved you if you had trusted me Sara. Instead, you made a whore of yourself with a mortal. I may forgive you still, but only if you obey me, now and always. But the mortal will suffer for your sins, I have ensured this."

"NO!" Sara automatically places herself between Joseph and Julian. She cannot allow any harm to befall him, it would be a sword through her own heart. "You will not hurt him. You cannot, you are an angel. What is wrong with you? Why are you doing this to us? You don't..." She shakes her head, her dark locks bouncing. "You don't love me, I know you don't... and I certainly do not love you. Why can't you just let me go? Please, just let me go."

Julian takes another stride closer, moving out of the light, becoming a stark black silhouette once again. "I... will... NEVER let you go Sara! This filth will never touch you again, nor will any other but I. Do you understand? You belong to ME! YOU ARE MINE!" He screams, snarls, completely lost to his rage. "You have made a fatal mistake Sara. One you will regret dearly... and so will HE!"

A blinding flash of light fills the room and there is the crash of thunder. Sara screams and tries to shield Joseph's body with her own. Her eyes are squeezed shut so hard that all she sees are spots. Fear and adrenaline pump through her. She waits for whatever retribution Julian has in store for them and begins to tremble.

"Hrrmmm... whas wrong..?" Joseph's sleepy voice slurs from below her.

Raising her head, she scans the room frantically. It's dark, and... it's empty.

"Sara, wha-"

"Oh Lord Joseph! Oh Lord!" She throws herself on him again. This time with the intention of hugging him forever. "I promise I will never let anyone hurt you. NEVER!"

"Sara..." He puts his arms around her and blinks away his haze of slumber. "First of all, that's my line. Second of all... you're kind of suffocating me." He lets out a mock wheeze.

"Oh!" She loosens her bear hug.

He lifts her head and kisses her so gently that she almost cries. "Please, please Sara, tell me what's wrong."

She kisses him then looks into his eyes. When she steadies her breath, she begins. "Why can't the world just disappear? Heaven, hell, all of it. Why can't there be nothing but you and me. I love you so much Joseph, but I've put you in such danger."

This causes him to sit up. "What are you talking about? Did that demon get into your dreams again? Ardat? Did she threaten us again?"

"No, no. It wasn't her, it was..." She pauses, her expression changing. "Wait a minute, I NEVER told you her name."

"Didn't you? Are you sure..? Oh... uh, well..." With a great deal of reluctance, Joseph tells her of his own encounters with the tiny demon and all that she said to him.

"Lord! How could you Joseph? How could you keep this from me?"

"I'm sorry, but I didn't want to worry you. I mean, you have enough to worry about already right?" He tries to pull her close but she pushes him away with a surprising strength.

"Joseph, we said we would face everything together, but you kept this from me, even as you made love to me. I... my heart... hurts."

"I'm sorry Sara. I told myself I was protecting you... and..." He drops his head.

"And what?" She asks tersely, although a hint of empathy is hidden in her eyes.

"...I was afraid."

"Of Ardat?"

"No! God no." He raises his head. "I was so afraid you would try to leave me again, to try and protect me. I know I'm selfish Sara, but I need you. I can't lose you. I love you."

Instantly her anger is gone and her heart overflows with love, she kisses his forehead. "I love you too Joseph. I guess I'm selfish too, because I need you even more. I couldn't ever leave you. Not now. You are inside me, inside my heart. I need you to breathe. Never ever think I will leave you... even if it's safer if I did. I can't." She sees him smile at her and his eyes glisten. "BUT... we need to always be honest with each other. Never hide things. We are in danger, both of us. So we need to depend on each other, we need to trust each other. It's you and me against heaven and hell, not simply one demon."

"Yes Sara, I swear. I won't keep anything from you again." His hand rests on her cheek and she nuzzles into it. "So, if it wasn't Ardat that got you freaked out, what was it? I mean what could possibly be worse than a demon with a vendetta?"

Suddenly Sara looks older, more mature, worldly, and Joseph can easily believe that she is over a thousand years old. She sighs, "I'm sorry Joseph. I guess I haven't told you everything either." She takes his hand. "We have a lot to talk about… this is going to take a while."

Joseph squeezes her hand, flashes a melancholy smile, and cocks one eyebrow. "I'm not going anywhere."

* * * * * * * * * *

Chapter 13

Fate Finds Us All

By the time the first light of day makes an appearance, Sara and Joseph have been talking for hours. Their conversation has moved from the bedroom to the breakfast bar. Both were famished, so Sara threw on Joseph's bathrobe and he pulled on a pair of briefs. While they continued to talk, Joseph whipped up a big batch of blueberry pancakes.

"Cooking relaxes me." He explained. "Especially cooking for someone... special." He blushed a bit saying this. Sara thought it was adorable. She knew she was only falling deeper and deeper in love with him.

During their long talk, Sara left no detail out, no matter how difficult. She laid out her intended bonding with Julian. As well as assuring Joseph that it was not out of love, but rather the process of heavenly politics. Julian was the highest ranking soldier of heaven and as the daughter of heaven's steward, it was appropriate that she bond with him. Julian had lobbied for their pairing almost from the day she came into existence.

Sara's parents allowed her the time she wished before she accepted her obligation. That was the way she always viewed her relationship with Julian, an obligation.

She recounted for him the insane possessiveness Julian displayed towards her of late. Not to mention his intent to harm Joseph because of their blossoming relationship.

"So... we've got a demon who wants to kill me, and use you for... something? And we have an angel who wants to kill me so he can have you for himself. Excellent! Good times!" He sarcastically sums up their situation over his massive stack of pancakes.

"Except he will never… have… me, no matter what he thinks or does. My heart is yours Joseph."

He leans over and kisses her. "And mine is yours Sara."

She tastes syrup, sweet on his lips. Grabbing him for another kiss, she lets her tongue enjoy the flavor. She could kiss him forever, she could feel his breath on her cheek forever, she could love him forever.

"Do you think he'll send one of those dog things after me?" Joseph asks as he carves out his next mouthful of pancakes.

Sara slices off her own impressive bite while answering. "No, angels have no control over the creatures of hell."

When he puts a little thought to it, he realizes that should have been pretty obvious, even to him. "Right. I guess that makes sense."

"If he truly means to do you harm, I don't know what he could do. No angel can harm a human without the will of the Lord."

"Or maybe they just haven't tried." He posits. "Is there really anything stopping him?"

Sara makes a face that says, she's not sure. "I just know that it has never happened. Any angel that defied the Lord or betrayed divinity was cast into hell, and there have not been that many. But none has ever dared to attack a mortal, none ever had any reason to. I don't know what would happen, and I don't believe he does either."

"Then hopefully he's just being a gigantic douche and talking out of his ass." He tries his best to ease her fears, if he can.

The look of dread on her face only lessens slightly. "Maybe, but Julian is not the sort to make idle threats. If he says something… he does it. He doesn't let things go."

"Yeah, so you told me." It's clear that the dark mood will not go away so easily. They eat silently for some time until he broaches the subject again. "What do you think Ardat wants you to do?"

"I can't do anything for her. I'm only a mortal now, remember?" She sounds annoyed.

Joseph's natural curiosity and hatred of any unanswered question has shifted his mind into overdrive. "She obviously thinks you can." He persists.

Sara huffs. "Maybe she wants to ransom me, try to force my father to do something for her... not that he would."

"But if that was the case, wouldn't she just grab you? Why does she want to convince you to-"

"I don't know Joseph! Everyone is against us! That's all I know, and I'm nothing but a human, I can't protect us! They can do anything to us. They can kill us whenever they wish. They can taunt and torture us at their leisure and I'm completely powerless to stop them!" Her hands are clenched, shaking on the breakfast bar, causing her plate to rattle noticeably.

Joseph reaches out. "It's okay, it's okay." He lays his hands over top of hers and the quaking subsides. "I'm sorry Sara. I'm still trying to get a grip on everything that's going on. It helps me to talk and hear everything out loud so we can try to figure out some options. I don't want to upset you."

Sara fights to calm herself, not so easy as when she had the grace of an angel. "I know Joseph, I'm sorry too. I shouldn't get angry with you. I know you're only trying to help, but I don't see anything we can do. This is all my fault, and we might have to pay the price together. I'm sorry."

"You have to stop blaming yourself for everything Sara! I mean if God really never wanted the angels to interfere on earth again, then he could have just made it impossible for them to do it. Am I right? So why leave them the possibility at all?"

"We, angel, human or demon, are given our choices to make. Those choices and the consequences of them make us who we are." She counters.

Joseph doesn't know what more to say and again they fall silent, a dark pall settling over them. After finishing breakfast, they are in a daze, moving to the couch and staring blankly at the TV. Even with remote in hand, Joseph isn't paying any attention to what's on. The last thing he clicked on was an episode of Deadliest Catch. Now there's some sort of ridiculously cheesy ghost hunting show on with guys wandering in a dark house constantly whispering "did you hear that?". The only thing he can focus on, the only thing he's thinking about, is how he can keep Julian away from Sara.

It's not unfair to say that jealousy was a big part of Joseph's feelings when Sara told him of Julian's intent to bond with her. It's easy enough to tell yourself that everyone has an ex, but it's a little different when that ex is some kind of divine being. How could anyone compete with that? It's like Jimmy Olsen having a crush on Lois Lane while Superman is flying her around Metropolis. But despite of that, Sara left no doubt in his mind of her feelings. He trusts her with his heart implicitly, perhaps foolishly, but he does. The more she shared with him, the more obvious it was that Julian did not deserve her. His only feeling towards Julian now is the concern over just how unhinged and dangerous he might be.

How the hell am I supposed to protect the woman I love from some psychotic angel?

Beside Joseph, Sara is also paying absolutely no attention to the TV. Due to the stress they're under and a deep exhaustion, her body is rebelling and demanding rest. Her eyelids droop repeatedly, until it's impossible to keep them open. Sara's eyes close, and for a few seconds there is a quiet, dark, peaceful oblivion.

Then Sara is beneath a brilliant blue sky, walking hand in hand with Joseph. The soft breeze smells of autumn and they are surrounded by an unending meadow. There is lush green grass for as far as the eye can see, and in the distance stands one great maple tree, tall and wide. It's leaves are glorious hues of red and gold.

She is dressed in a fine white summer dress. A beautiful regency style gown that could have fit in perfectly during the age of any Jane Austen novel. Joseph is wearing a crisp, white collared shirt with tan trousers. They look like characters one might find in a Monet painting from long bygone days. She can imagine Joseph with brush in hand, capturing this moment on canvas.

It's an idilic setting and a perfect feeling. Joseph's green eyes sparkle in the sunlight, even though there is no sun present in the wide blue sky. He squeezes her hand and raises it to his lips, kissing it like a gentleman of romance and chivalry. She loves how he showers affection on her, how he radiates such deep emotion. He makes her feel like the most precious thing in existence.

A chill wind rises suddenly, harsh and bracing. Sara has to close her eyes against the sting of the unexpected gale. In her grasp, Joseph's hand becomes ice cold. Opening her eyes, she finds the blue sky gone. Darkness has descended, and with it... death.

The once lush green meadow is nothing but filth, rot, and decay. The tree in the distance is gnarled and twisted, transformed into a nightmare shape, a scream taken form.

"S... Sara..?" The voice beside her is weak and strained. His cold hand slips from her grasp and Joseph crumples to the ground at her feet.

Sara's throat is shredded by her scream. Dropping to her knees, she groans from the effort of rolling him over onto his back. He's like a dead weight and it's a strain to move him at all. His skin is clammy and sallow, but most terrifying is the sight of a dark red stain on his pristine white shirt.

"Oh Lord. No! No!!"

The spot of red, directly over his heart, is spreading rapidly. She frantically presses her bare hands against the wound, trying to staunch the bleeding. She might as well be trying to plug a hole in a dam. The warm fluid continues to flow between and over her fingers unabated. She screams uselessly for help, her voice cracking and failing, already knowing there is no one to hear her. Joseph's clothes and Sara's hands are soaked in his blood. It pools on the decayed earth all around them, staining her dress a dark crimson.

"S... ara, I lov..." He doesn't finish. With a rattling breath, the life drains from Joseph's body.

All Sara can do is cradle him in her arms and cry uncontrollably. She rocks his lifeless body, repeating the word "no". On some level she knows that this is all a dream, but all of her senses contradict that fact. For her, the man she loves, the ONLY person she has ever loved in this way, lies dead in her arms. All that made him Joseph Ross is gone. She watched him die. Watched the spark leave his eyes. A pointless mortal death like billions of others... but to her he was like no one else.

He was hers. He was her true love.

She continues to rock him, sobbing. By cupping his face, her hands leave it smeared with blood. She screams his name, shakes him, squeezes him to her breast, anything except accept that he is gone.

"It doesn't need to end this way, you know."

Sara snaps her head up to see Ardat standing above her. "YOU DID THIS!" She shrieks at the demon.

"I'm sorry, but this is your dream Sara, your fears of what will come. I had to show you, but I did not bring this about, I didn't create it. However, I'll dispel it from your mind for now." The demon makes a small gesture with her pale hand. The body of Joseph Ross fades into nothingness, leaving Sara's arms empty. The landscape fades as well, turning into an unremarkable, windowless grey room. Sara, still on her knees, is cleansed of the blood stains that had covered her. Her clothing has changed into the simple mortal garb that Joseph bought for her.

She stares at her empty hands and rage boils over inside her, an explosion that, were she still an angel, could have wrought untold destruction. Like a berserk animal, she lets out a tortured wail and lunges at Ardat. Her hands are like talons, aiming for the demon's throat.

As fast as a thought, Ardat's uncommonly dark shadow springs to life. The black mass stretches out into two hands, catching Sara by the wrists. Her attack halted, she is left dangling in the air.

"I understand that you can't bring yourself to trust a demon, but a time will come where you may have to, or else you could lose everything."

"What do you want from me?" Sara spits out.

A look of sadness overtakes Ardat. "Nothing. Not anymore. I guess you could say my eyes have been opened. It wasss..." she chuckles grimly, "a very harsh light after being in the dark for so long. Painful, but necessary."

"What... what are you talking about?"

"Sara?" Joseph's voice booms and echoes through the empty room and Ardat's shadow form releases Sara. She drops to her feet as the room around them begins to rattle and break apart.

Just before the dreamscape is erased, Ardat calls out desperately, "When we meet again we'll both face a terrible choice... a sacrifice!"

"Sara. Can you hear me? Are you okay?" Joseph nudges her shoulders and her eyes struggle to open. "You were kind of talking in your sleep. It looked a little scary... like something bad was going down."

"Joseph!" She throws her arms around him. "I love you."

He chuckles. "I love you too, but you didn't really answer my question. Are you okay? Did you have a bad dream?"

She nods. "Very bad."

"Need to talk about it?"

Sara considers it, but she can't bring herself to put words to what she just went through... not yet. "Can I have a little time? I can't talk about it quite yet. Please trust me Joseph."

He takes her hand, kissing the back of it and reminding Sara of her dream. "If that's what you need." He says. "I do trust you Sara, completely." A day ago he certainly would have felt slighted, but now his trust in her is steadfast. She's opened up so much in the last twenty-four hours, he will not begrudge her the time she needs. "Whenever you're ready, I'm all ears."

"Thank you Joseph. I mean it. Thank you for everything." She snuggles in and rests her head on his shoulder. Even at a time like this, it still makes her heart light. It makes her feel that they can overcome anything as long as they're together. That might be the farthest thing from reality, but her love is so strong, she could almost believe it.

Morning passes to afternoon and afternoon passes to evening. To keep from going utterly stir crazy, Joseph broke out his sketchpad again. He considered trying to paint but found that his oils had dried up and his brushes had turned brittle. Instead, he sits on the floor drawing Sara's portrait as she poses, somewhat uncomfortably, on the couch.

A question nagged at her when Joseph said he wanted to draw her. *Does he see me the same way he saw his old girlfriend?* She managed to stave off these needles of insecurity. She decided to return the trust he has placed in her, as well as trusting in her own heart. Her strange and mysterious heart unquestioningly feels Joseph's love for her.

A blush colors her cheeks under his studious gaze. The only sounds in the room are the light scrapes of pencil on paper and Sara's nervously flustered breath.

A sudden knock on the door causes her to jump and let out a tiny shriek. Both of them stare anxiously at the door without uttering a breath, let alone a sound.

"Helloo-ooo?" A creaky and sugary sweet voice carries through the door.

"Marjorie?" Sara replies.

She moves to rise but Joseph gestures for her to stay put. He lays his sketchpad on the coffee table and walks to the door. Leaving the chain on, he opens it a crack.

"Um, hi Marjorie." It's still weird for him to call her that. "It's not really the best time... what can we do for you?"

His neighbor's innocently smiling face can be seen through the narrow opening. It's deeply lined from a long, full life, but the brown eyes behind her thin glasses are still vibrant and energetic. They are certainly not the eyes of a woman whose mind or faculties have dulled from age. He had never bothered to notice before.

"Oh I'm such an airhead! My prescription ran out and I completely forgot to go to the pharmacy before it got dark. Could you please walk an old woman to the store? I just don't feel safe going alone. I hate to impose, but I need my pills before I go to bed."

Joseph hems and haws. "Couldn't they deliver it for you?" Sara has joined him at the door, standing at his side.

"Not until tomorrow and I need my pills tonight or I could faint dead away! I know I'm being such a terrible bother but the store closes in a couple hours. If you can't... I guess I'll have to go by myself... I just hope I don't run into any of those street gangs or druggies..."

Joseph sighs as Sara makes a little sympathetic murmur. "Um, just give us a minute, okay Marjorie?" He doesn't wait for her to agree, he closes the door and turns to Sara. "I can see if my car will start, I'll take her and come right back. You stay here."

"What!?" From the way Sara's jaw is clenched and the determination in her eyes... the word 'uncompromising' would be an understatement. "Absolutely not! I am not staying behind. If you go, I go. Together... remember?"

It's clear this is an argument he will not win. "Yes..." he nods, "together." Bending down slightly, he kisses her tenderly on her soft, red lips before opening the door again.

Mrs. Jackson stands with her hands clasped in front of her and her brows arched inquiringly.

"Okay Marjorie, we can give my car a try. If it doesn't start then we'll need to walk."

"Oh thank you. I know I'm such a bother, that's why my boys never visit. You two are so sweet. Thank you."

"It's fine Marjorie." He assures her. "We'll be right out."

When he closes the door again, Sara clenches his hand in a death grip. "Joseph, I have such a bad feeling about this! We shouldn't be going out. We definitely shouldn't be going out at night."

He curls his free hand around hers protectively. "I know, but come on, the bottom line is, we can't stay in here forever. I have a job and we need to live our life. Besides, I don't think a chain on the door is going to keep out any supernatural beings if they wanted in. So really, we aren't any safer in here than out there, right?" Sara nods with great reluctance. "We need to face whatever's going to come at us. Whether it's tonight, tomorrow, next week, if it's gonna happen it's gonna happen. We can't avoid it."

"I know. You're right Joseph. Whatever happens, you know I love you."

They embrace and he places a kiss softly on her forehead. "I know, and I love you too Sara."

After donning shoes and jackets, Joseph grabs his car keys. The key chain bears the words 'pray for a miracle' a personal joke that refers to starting his beloved junker. Hand in hand, they head out the door to join Marjorie.

The elderly woman gives Sara a hug unexpectedly. "I'll treat you both to a chocolate bar for putting you out like this."

"That's okay Marjorie, really. Just remember, my car might not start. It isn't very reliable." Joseph reminds her.

"Oh that's fine. If we need to walk, we need to walk. It's no difference to me, I've walked this earth since the dawn of time. I've put so many miles on these two feet, I'm happy to put on as many more as I can before my last day comes."

"Okay..." His eyes connect with Sara's. The lover's hands are still linked, fingers interlocking as if crafted to fit together perfectly. He feels such remarkable strength in her, as if nothing could break them apart. They both take a deep breath... "Ready?"

"Yes, let's go." Sara speaks with all the courage she has, while Ardat's words reverberate through her mind.

When we meet again we will both face a terrible choice... a sacrifice.

A sacrifice.

* * * * * * * *

Chapter 14

With The Edge Of A Sword

Mrs. Jackson, Sara, and Joseph make their way to the rear stairs of the apartment building which leads to its small outdoor parking lot. This was how Joseph brought Sara to his modest abode on that first night. She remembers how he found her, alone and scared out of her mind. He had to help her climb these concrete stairs. Her legs were so unsteady that she had to cling to him for support. Such a short while ago, yet it feels like she's lived a lifetime since then.

Has it truly been only three days?

She's astounded by her mortal perception of time, her eyes no longer peering into the eternal as the angels do. In a different situation, she might have had a wry laugh, thinking about her unbelievable change of circumstances. But right now she feels a palpable sense of danger. She's on high alert and watchful for anything that could be hiding in the dark.

In the far corner of the lot sits Joseph's mustard yellow and rust spotted VW beetle. As he descends the stairs, he mutters a prayer to the automotive gods to help the old girl start.

The overhead lamps in the parking lot cast sufficient light on most nights, but tonight there is an eerie silvery haze hanging in the air. The night itself feels... wrong. Sara is latched to Joseph's hand so tightly she threatens to cut off the circulation to his fingers.

Behind them, Mrs. Jackson is moving down the steps at a snail's pace. "I'm afraid stairs are not my friends these days. Did I ever tell you about my hip replacement?"

"Uh, no. I don't think you did." Joseph tries, unsuccessfully, to remain patient with her. "Look, I'll go ahead and try to start the car."

Sara tries to protest, but he's already let go of her hand and is bounding down the last few steps. He tries to race across the parking lot, but as soon as he is separated from Sara, the ominous darkness around him begins to shift and stir.

"Joseph stop!" She shouts, but he's already well into the lot before he spots the dark shapes stretching, warping, and reaching for each other. Every shadows in the vicinity is drawn into a large mass. It covers the pavement between he and Sara, separating them. A strange black hole of sorts forms from the shadows, swirling around a central point.

Joseph doesn't move an inch, he feels a river of ice water run through his veins, he slowly turns his head. Behind him, something is rousing in the eye of the shadowy hurricane. A ghostly pale figure in tattered black jeans and a sex pistols t-shirt rises from darkness. Ardat's youthful face and beetle black eyes form an inscrutable mask, but she is squarely focused on him.

"You stay the fuck away from him!" There is no panic in Sara's voice. It's not shrill or quavering. Instead, it's filled with a hardened strength that has long been hidden within her heart. That strength has finally been given voice, thanks in part to her love for Joseph.

Sara wants to rush at the small demon but the frail hand of Mrs. Jackson has taken hold of her arm. Before she can free herself of the old woman's grip, Ardat raises one hand towards her.

A tendril of shadow fires out from the whirlpool at Ardat's feet. Mimicking it's master, it forms a huge black hand. The hand wraps itself solidly around Sara all the way from her waist to her shoulders, trapping her on the spot. The vise like grip of the demon's servant shadow is impossible to break. Mrs. Jackson steps back from Sara, merely observing all which is unfolding. Joseph's unassuming neighbor does not appear to be shocked in the slightest by what she is witnessing.

"Joseph, RUN!" Sara cries out, but he is already charging hard towards Ardat, desperate to rescue the woman he loves. He would run through the very gates of hell for Sara. He would die for her.

He roars like a senseless beast as anger and emotion control him, rendering his judgment questionable at best. All he knows is that he has to save Sara. He played cornerback on the football team in high school and he falls back on those instincts now. However, taking down a wide receiver is nothing like trying to tackle a creature of hell... needless to say.

Ardat raises her other hand towards him. As with Sara, a dark tendril erupts from her storm of shadows. This time, the powerful hand takes Joseph by the throat and lifts him off the ground. He sputters and strains immediately as the unearthly hand slowly crushes his windpipe. His fingers pry and scrape uselessly against this dark power. It's the only thing he can do to fight for his life, and it's about as effective as trying to bend steel with his bare hands.

Still helplessly bound by Ardat, Sara is roiling with fury. "LET HIM GO YOU BITCH!" She hollers. Watching Joseph struggling for breath, his fingers clawing, legs kicking, her rage quickly turns to fear and bargaining. "Alright! Whatever you want! I'll do whatever you want! I swear, just let him go! Please."

Ardat's black eyes can't hide the conflict within. "No... you were right before little bird." She lets out a single sad, defeated laugh. "There is nothing you can do for me. Isn't that right... old woman?" Ardat looks over at Mrs. Jackson standing near the stairs.

Marjorie makes a soft tsk sound, as if disappointed but not surprised.

Sara twists her neck to look at the old woman. "Marjorie?" Confusion and bewilderment are added onto the thousand other emotions overwhelming the fallen angel.

"I've made my choice!" Ardat shouts in a faltering voice. "I can't go back. I can't. I can't." She keeps repeating this over and over through gritted teeth.

Mrs. Jackson's drops her head slightly. "I understand dearie. Your burden has been a heavy one indeed. Often something we see as a punishment, is meant to be a task, a test, an opportunity to rise up again. I've certainly been accused of testing too much, and too harshly. I'm truly sorry Ardat. None of us is infallible."

Sara is as confused as she is frightened. Joseph has turned a disturbing shade of red. The veins in his temples can be easily seen even from where she is being held. He doesn't have much time left.

"Shut up!" Ardat snaps at Marjorie.

"Please Ardat..." Sara summons the willpower to calm herself. All she can do is implore, beg, the fallen angel turned demon to spare his life. "It's not too late. Please, if you were ever an angel then you must understand that those with power are honor bound to protect those without. His name is Joseph Ross, he is a good man and... I love him. I don't know if there is a divine plan, I don't know what hand fate will play, I only know in my heart that it is not his place to die like this. It is not his time. Please don't do this."

Joseph's legs have gone still and his hands are weakly shaking.

"She's right. It's not too late Ardat... what path will you take?" Marjorie asks.

"FUCK!" Ardat howls furiously.

Sara feels the shadowy hand release her and watches Joseph drop hard to the ground at the same time. She races past Ardat, not giving the demon a single thought. Reaching Joseph as he lay on the ground, she throws her arms around him. He is coughing and gasping for air, but he is alive. She helps him scrabble to his knees.

"Lord! Joseph, can you hear me? Are you alright? Can you breathe?" She peppers him with as many questions as kisses.

"I'm... okay." He assures her through a painfully bruised throat.

She continues to kiss him even as he fights to stand. He is weakened, but he needs to be on his feet for her.

She helps support him. "Lord, I love you so much. I was so scared. I thought I was going to lose you." The two are lost in each other, completely forgetting about Mrs. Jackson and Ardat.

The tempest of shadows at the demon's feet has quelled. Only the lone black silhouette of the teenaged girl with the ashen skin and uneven blonde hair remains. It mirrors her exactly, as any normal shadow should.

Ardat walks slowly towards the elderly black woman waiting near the steps. Mrs. Jackson stands her ground, sympathy brimming in her hazel eyes. A few feet apart, they face each other. Inky black liquid burns Ardat's cheeks as it runs from her eyes.

"Do I really have to go back? There isn't any other way? You can't..." The sad young woman tilts her head and holds a hand out.

Mrs. Jackson shakes her head almost imperceptibly. "I'm only an old woman. I can't do anything for you dearie, except tell you how very proud I am, and that it has never, NEVER, been wings that make an angel divine. Remember that dearie, never forget it, never forget."

At that, a demon from hell smiles a smile filled with grace, love, and beauty.

There is a blinding flash and a deafening crack of thunder. Everyone in the vicinity is robbed of their sight momentarily as lightning splits the skies. It takes only a few seconds for their vision to return, but it's long enough. The first thing Marjorie sees, is a gleaming sword tip, protruding from the center of Ardat's chest. The smile on her black lips is gone, and a gurgle is the only sound she makes.

"Julian!" Sara screams in horror as she continues to help hold Joseph up. Across the parking lot she can only see those familiar glittering golden wings. They fully block her view of Marjorie and Ardat, but somehow Sara knows exactly what has happened.

Julian, the honored soldier of heaven, stands behind his sister with his sword buried in her back nearly to the hilt. Then, making one quick swipe, he wrenches the weapon free of it's victim.

Ardat's dips her head, staring at her chest. Marjorie sheds a single tear, and Ardat slumps to the pavement.

Julian virtually spits at her. "Fool! Dear sister. Proving again that you are as useless as you are stupid. Return to hell vile creature, and should it ever regurgitate you, you will taste the edge of my blade again, as many times as it must!"

He takes no notice of Mrs. Jackson whatsoever. Or if he does, he doesn't care enough to bother giving her a glance. Laying at his feet, the body of his sister blackens and cracks. Ardat turns to charcoal, then to cinders, and then to ash, to be blown away on the breeze.

"You bastard!" Sara screams. "How could you!?" Even now, her empathy for any and all is fully evidenced.

Julian spins on her. Lightning crackles in his eyes, his hair, his wings. Rage is not sufficient to describe the darkness inside him, it's closer to pure hatred, or even madness. With one beat of his great wings, he closes the distance between them. Sara can barely recognize him in the throes of this almost demonic insanity.

"Apostate!" He roars. The back of his hand lashes out and strikes her in the cheek with a loud crack. She is sent flying and lands in a heap on the ground several feet away.

Joseph shouts something incoherent. His own pain is completely forgotten. His blood is boiling with anger, he wants to hurt Julian... he wants to kill him. His clenched fist flies, aimed squarely at the tall angel's jaw. Though it connects heavily, solidly, it is Joseph who howls in pain. Julian doesn't flinch in the slightest.

As Joseph grabs at his bruised hand, Julian takes hold of him by the hair. Over two thousand years of building hatred and resentment boils over within Julian, and he snaps.

"Who do you think you are?! WHAT do you think you are?!" He is holding Joseph nose to nose in front of his face. "I am the divine and you are a slug! You despoil me with the touch of your flesh just as you have despoiled Sara. You filth! How could our Lord ever favor you over his own children?! We were the first! Heaven was meant for the angels not for you. We were the divine creation! You are nothing but meat set to rot. I shall become the true Lord and dispel every single human soul from heaven... then I will bring my host to this realm and wipe out every last mortal on earth. You. Are. At. An. END!"

Joseph grunts and squirms, it feels like his scalp is being ripped from his head. Whether from of the pain or something else entirely, he is suddenly thinking with a laser focused clarity. He doesn't know if his hand is broken, but it's clear that a physical attack is utterly futile. There is only one thing he can think to do. One hail mary long shot that might at least save Sara, if it actually works.

Looking Julian straight in the eye... Joseph spits in his face.

The angel does in fact let go of Joseph's hair, dropping him, he even staggers back a few steps as if gravely injured. Then lightning explodes all around him. Julian screams like a rabid creature, high pitched and manic. He raises his heavenly sword, it's lethal tip meant for Joseph's mortal heart.

Do it... Joseph thinks to himself, and spreads his arms wide, offering no defense, no resistance.

Julian lunges forward, but an instant before his sword can run Joseph through, something leaps between them.

"SARA!!!" Terror hits Joseph in the chest like a physical force. Her back is to him as she's facing Julian. Between her shoulder blades, visible through her dark, flowing hair, is the tip of a bloodstained sword.

"No... no..." Julian is also paralyzed by fear. The lightning in his eyes is gone, his cool blue pupils are staring into Sara's huge eyes. Her expression is one of shock and agony. He withdraws his sword with a sickening sound and Sara topples backwards.

Joseph catches her in his arms and carefully lowers her down, resting her against his body. "No no no no..." Blood already stains her jacket darkly and he can feel it running onto his legs beneath her. "Why Sara? It was supposed to be me... not you, it was supposed to be me."

Julian has gone deathly white and looks like he's about to throw up, if such a thing were possible.

Sara's hand rises weakly to Joseph's cheek. "I had to. I'm sorry Joseph. It was... my price to pay... not yours." Her eyelids flutter, her pupils are unfocused. "Couldn't let... hurt you..."

He kisses her forehead. "It's alright Sara. You'll be okay... you'll be okay. I need you Sara. I need you."

She almost smiles, her lip quivering.

Slowly, Mrs. Jackson approaches the tragic scene. She quietly walks up behind Julian who still can't bring himself to move.

"'m sorry Joseph... w-wanted to stay... with y-you forever..."

Salty droplets rain on her face. Tears falling straight from Joseph's anguished heart baptize her. "I love you Sara. Please don't leave me, please don't leave."

"I'm sorry. Shhhh... don't cry... you made me... so..." Her hand slips from his cheek, her eyes close, and suddenly she is floating, looking down on her own body. Joseph is in so much pain, his face is frozen in a rictus of intense grief. His tears are suspended in the air, unmoving. Nearby, Julian is also stock still. Looking around, the floating Sara discovers that everything has halted, time itself has stopped. There is no sound, no motion, nothing.

She casts her eyes on her mortal body, embraced by Joseph, eyes closed, it's life snuffed out. The floating Sara holds her hands up and they shine with an ethereal light, along with the rest of her form. She is very familiar with this phenomenon from the countless mortals she and the other angels would greet at the gates of heaven. This is her soul self. Her mortal existence has come to an end.

"I'm dead." She says plainly.

"Yes dearie, I'm afraid so."

Sara is suitably stunned to not only see Marjorie walking towards her while the rest of existence is in stasis, but that Joseph's neighbor can obviously see and hear her as well!

"Marjorie?! How can... what is happening? Are, are you doing this? How...?" Her confusion is well warranted. No mortal can see a departing soul self, regardless of what some con artists and charlatans might claim. This time freeze is also unprecedented as far as Sara knows. Normally a soul simply moves on, ascends or descends, this is all highly unusual.

"Oh no dearie. I can't do anything like this. You could say I have some connections though. Friends in high places. This..." Her withered hands gesture around at the world held still in time. "Well, we felt you deserved a small gift for your sacrifice. This is all we can give you child, just a moment in time."

Sara's soul self drifts down to Marjorie. After a glance at Joseph behind her, she turns back to the now thoroughly mysterious woman. "But, aren't you mortal? I don't understand this, and who is we?"

Mrs. Jackson wobbles her head from side to side. "Mmm... mortal? Yes... but not exactly." She hesitates. "Things have gotten so mixed up. I guess a lot of that is my fault, but I couldn't just up and tell everyone everything could I? That would make freewill pointless. Folks need to find their own path, make their own choices. All these people that just follow blindly instead of finding their own way. So many wrong ideas out there, even in heaven. It gets hard for me to watch and yet I'm powerless to step in. So I let myself forget who I am until I need to remember again. Sounds silly, and selfish, but it's the only way I could survive. But as I said, even if I could step in, I wouldn't, I did it once, broke the rules, but never again, and that is ever MY burden."

Sara is struggling to piece together these cryptic and disjointed words. Then an impossible thought forms in her mind. "You're..." Her eyes grow huge and her shimmering hands rise to her mouth in astonishment.

Mrs. Jackson nods modestly. "The Mother and the Father, the beginning and the end." Then she waves her hand dismissively. "And yet, I'm also none of these."

"My Lord." Sara utters with reverence and awe.

This time Marjorie shakes her head with a tut-tut sound. "Some two thousand years ago, but I became mortal as the sacrifice, and that is what I have been ever since. I'm just Marjorie, same as I've been Richard and Aziza and Kyung and Gianna and Steven and Ekaterina, and hundreds more before. I am mortal... but, I'm eternal too. A cycle of beginning and end and beginning. Mortal yes, but never truly parted from the divine, just like you Sara."

"Then you ARE doing this?"

"No, no. I am only an old woman who can see things. Exactly what I told you. This moment is a gift from your father. A bit of rule bending on his part, but then you can't blame a father for loving his daughter."

Sara is on the verge of tears. "Why is all of this happening? Was it always going to end this way? Were Joseph and I doomed from the first? I don't want to leave him! Why? Why does it have to be this way?"

"Oh dearie, why does a mother give birth? To create, to give life, to pass on that perfect love to a new shining light in the universe. But, she also knows that that bright light will have to find its own way in time. She will love it and nurture it, but she knows she can't control it, can't keep it hidden away. You give what you can to them, teach them, and then trust in them. That's all a mother can do. Heaven, hell, earth, this universe, they are ALL one in the same, and none of them are any more or less than what our children make of them." She smiles kindly. "I know, I know, I talk in circles. Old habits I'm afraid. Now, your time is short dearie, your father gave this moment to you so you could say goodbye. He was harsh in his punishment, but he also made darn sure you had someone to watch over you… your sentinel, your protector."

"He sent me to Joseph?"

"Mm-hmm, you see, for a few of us, some paths are visible for a while even though their destination is not. You needed Joseph and he needed you. Two hearts that called to each other even before meeting. It wasn't so much your father sending you to him, as it was you being drawn to him. Your father simply had to let you go. You were supposed to find each other Sara. A few things truly are meant to be."

"But, but now I have to leave him." She looks down at her iridescent hands with sadness.

"For now, yes. This existence isn't eternal, not here. But your love will be. You know that in your heart don't you dearie? You feel it? A true love will have pain, it will have goodbyes, but it doesn't end. Even as you move on, a part of him is within you Sara." Her hazel eyes exude kindness and warmth. "Now, you need to say goodbye child."

Sara nods and turns to Joseph. She kneels before him. There is such terrible suffering written on his face. She wishes she could take it from him, but she knows she can't. He will live on, he is mortal and mortals must endure the pain of goodbyes.

Her shimmering hand rests on his cheek. She brushes away a teardrop with her thumb. "You are so beautiful Joseph. You gave me hope when all hope was lost. You gave me safe harbour in your arms and in your heart. I felt so much love, such a pure, unconditional love. You gave me a lifetime of love in these few days we had together. I love you Joseph. You will ever hold my heart, wherever you may go, and I shall ever hold yours. Please have a happy life. I'm going to be watching, I want you to live and laugh..." Her voice cracks. "...and love." She blinks as though she were crying, a reflex of sorts since her soul self cannot shed tears. "Goodbye Joseph. I will always love you. Always."

Her hands on his cheeks, she kisses his forehead as he had done for her on so many instances. She remembers how it made her feel safe and loved every single time.

Then Sara stands and turns away from him. She is face to face with the mannequin-like Julian. "What will happen to him?" She asks Marjorie.

Mrs. Jackson tilts her head a bit, her eyes are sad. "He chose his path. There are consequences to every choice we make, as you know. Some good and some bad. His consequences will NOT be good." She smiles at Sara. "You still have understanding, still feel kindness, even for one who wronged you so badly?"

"I guess I can see now how easy it is to be swayed by your feelings."

"From your time here?" Marjorie asks.

"Uh-huh, but even as an angel, I was always quick to follow my feelings instead of my head. I don't think the angels are really as divine as they like to believe."

Marjorie raises her eyebrows. "Now I wouldn't necessarily say that... they just need to understand, that we are all one, we are not different or separated, we are ALL a part of the divine. No one better than the other." She gives Sara a wink.

A dazzling light appears from the sky, shining brightly on Sara's soul self. She can hear her mother's voice welcoming her home and as she begins to ascend, she asks Marjorie one last question.

"What will I become now?"

The elderly woman smiles broadly. "Oh dear child, exactly what you've always been.... an angel."

Joseph cradles Sara's body on his lap. He brushes the hair from her face, her eyes have closed, and her chest has gone still. "No! Please don't go Sara, please." There is a warm tingling on his cheeks and his forehead.

Marjorie stands before Julian, his bloodstained sword still in his hand. She shakes her head. "You closed your eyes Julian. You looked away and saw only yourself."

His eyes narrow. "Who?" Then his eyes fly open with an unbelievable realization. "My Lor-"

The word burns in his throat as he chokes on fire and ash. Collapsing to his knees, his sword bursts into flame, searing the flesh from his hand.

Flesh..? He stares in confusion at the charred, boney mess that was his right hand. The sword hilt clatters onto the ground beside him. The blade has completely disintegrated, leaving only the spotlessly gleaming silver and golden handle.

Julian isn't even afforded the luxury of screaming as his body burns from the inside out. His once magnificent wings molt and decompose in seconds, becoming rotted stumps sticking out from his trench coat.

He falls forward and his eyes bulge grotesquely a moment before his entire body lights aflame. He reaches his remaining hand out towards Marjorie, silently begging for mercy.

She looks away and cries, she can do nothing for him. Julian's body is fully consumed by the fire. It burns so hotly that the asphalt bubbles and liquefies beneath him.

Nearby, Joseph can feel the harsh intensity of the heat on his face and hands. Even now he tries to shield Sara's body with his own. As he does so, ribbons and flecks of light begin to dance all over her body. He no longer feels the heat of the nearby inferno. He feels... protected. His heart knows there is nothing remotely harmful in what is happening to Sara. There is only peace and light, a beautiful light, a heavenly light. The weight of her body on his legs is slowly diminishing. As the dancing lights glow brighter, Sara's mortal shell wavers and fades, her body transforming into starlight.

Marjorie puts a hand in front of her face as the hellfire that is devouring Julian dwindles away. When she looks again, there is nothing left but a deep, charred spot in the parking lot, and an exquisite sword hilt. All that was Julian, the greatest soldier of heaven, has been fully consumed in the flames of his betrayal. She whispers something into the wind then turns her back.

"Sara..." Joseph utters her name, no longer with sadness, but with such a deep love and gratitude. She continues to disappear in his arms. He watches the lights dim and he understands. She is returning home, and by knowing this, his own grief is tempered somewhat. Somehow he knows, this is not the end.

The tiny lights blink out one by one, and when the last is extinguished, Sara is gone.

The blood which stained his clothes and the ground has also disappeared. He sits on the cold pavement, silently staring at the stars overhead for a long while until Mrs. Jackson wanders over.

"What in the world are you doing down there?" She asks.

He gives his head a shake in stunned confusion, unsure he heard her strange question correctly. "What?"

"We need to hurry if we're going to get to the pharmacy before it closes."

"Are you serious?! You're thinking about your pills after what just happened?" He snaps.

Now it's Mrs. Jackson who looks genuinely confused, not to mention affronted. "You fell down. Tripped right over your own feet. You're young, I think you'll survive. Really! Making such a fuss… and don't bother about your car. It looks like you can use the walk!"

He gets to his feet. "What? I'm talking about Sara."

She eyes him curiously. "Sara? Who's Sara?"

Joseph stares hard at her, trying to spot any hint that she's feigning ignorance. He sees none. If she is acting, she is doing so masterfully.

"Well," She waves her hands impatiently. "Let's go. I need those pills." She claps like a school teacher bringing her class to attention.

His mouth is hanging open. "Uh... Uh... o-okay." He honestly doesn't know what else to do except go along with her.

"You're acting awfully strange tonight. You're not on the drugs are you? I hear all about those meth addicts and their labs everywhere, all over the city. I have the Fox news, I know what's going on!" She frowns at him suspiciously.

"What!? No, no, no. I'm not on drugs Marjor- uh, Mrs. Jackson."

Indescribably, there is a distinct sensation of reality resetting itself. Somehow the woman beside him is Mrs. Jackson again instead of Marjorie. Heaven and hell, the balance, everything is reset, everything back in order. He wonders if he is the only one who can feel it, and if so, why him.

Mrs. Jackson has moved on to rambling about the problems with young people today. Joseph glances behind them as they start walking. He can see a blackened circle of charred asphalt in the middle of the parking lot.

Mrs. Jackson admonishes him for not listening. She tells him how important manners are and blames the Internet for everyone's short attention span. As she carries on, Joseph raises his head and looks towards the heavens. He keeps on agreeing politely with everything Mrs. Jackson is saying without really listening.

A melancholy smile crosses his lips. He stares at the countless twinkling lights high above him. He knows logically those beautiful dots are stars, giant celestial fusion reactors that burn throughout the cold void of space. He knows the light he is marvelling at travels for decades if not hundreds of thousands of years to reach earth. A miracle of the universe, a miracle of nature. He knows all of this...

Yet, he also knows now that somewhere out there in the vastness of existence, there are other bright lights.

For he held the brightest of those lights in his arms for a time. It filled his life with starlight. It set fire to his soul. It gave him hope and it gave him purpose.

Joseph can still see that light, burning radiantly deep within his heart, his unwavering beacon.

Sara... his angel.

I love you Sara... always.

* * * * * * *

Epilogue

A very long six months have passed since that fateful night in the fall. Autumn turned to winter and winter to spring. Half a year since Sara gave her life for Joseph and by proxy, all of humanity.

The numerous media reports of gruesome killings by unknown animals ceased immediately afterward. However, none of the "animals" were ever captured or accounted for. In the ensuing six months, international tensions cooled somewhat from their previous boiling point. Although the rhetoric had died down, rebuilding the trust between nations might take years, if not decades. The rate of murders worldwide also rolled back to their normal but horrendous numbers. The brief but massive spike was written off as an aberration by pundits and so-called experts.

Closer to home, you couldn't have blamed Joseph if he had chalked up those unbelievable days with Sara to an overactive imagination. Not only did Mrs. Jackson flatly deny ever meeting Sara, but so did his Java Jolt co-workers. Jill even went so far as to joke that he was so hard up that he was inventing girlfriends. At this, she giggled a little more than what could be considered polite. The entire world had forgotten Sara... everyone but Joseph.

Despite whatever memory gaps those around him may have suffered, a few scraps of evidence did remain. There was the shallow, scorched hole in the parking lot of his building. The site of Julian's destruction is now filled in with limestone gravel. His attempts to interrogate Mrs. Jackson on the origin of the hole ended with a wave of her hand and her suggestion that lightning probably struck there.

But, in addition to this, resting on a shelf in Joseph's closet, there is an ornate silver and gold sword hilt, sans blade. The remnants of the mad angel's holy weapon, the weapon which took Sara's mortal life. Joseph retrieved it that night when he and Mrs. Jackson returned from the pharmacy. She dismissed it out of hand as a part of someone's Halloween costume. She told him about how her boys would dress as Power Rangers and play swords all the time. He didn't bother to argue.

In that same closet hang the clothes that Joseph bought for Sara to wear. They are a daily reminder to him of those incredible days that he holds dear to his heart. And proof positive that even a trip to Wal-Mart can be a romantic experience if it's with the right person.

Still more tangible evidence resides within Joseph's sketchbook. There is the drawing of Sara and Marjorie sitting and laughing in the park. On the next page, an unfinished sketch of Sara. Her hair is roughly outlined along with the shape of her face. The detail that he was able to complete and capture perfectly were her eyes. The stunning eyes that Joseph sees every time he closes his own. They are filled with love and worry, alive yet troubled, exactly as he remembers them. This was the sketch he had been drafting only minutes before Sara gave her life to save his.

Yet even without these clues, Joseph would never doubt for a second, the time he spent with Sara or the love he shared with her. In that moment when she passed on, he understood so much, he saw so much. The strange awareness of reality shifting on itself opened his eyes in totally new ways. He knew that Sara's sacrifice had re-forged the barricades protecting the mortal realm from hell. Sara, being both mortal and divine, as was her Lord before her, shed her blood and mortality to restore the balance, albeit a new balance. Everything was new, and only time would reveal all that had changed.

He knew all these things, he just didn't know HOW he knew them.

To this day, he can feel that deep and powerful connection to Sara. He has missed her immensely, but he also feels like she is not exactly gone. There have been many a hard night, where he would lay in the dark and be overwhelmed by grief or loneliness. There were nights when he could not hold back the tears. On those nights he would always feel a warm tingling on his cheek. He knew that his love for Sara would not wane. She lived, and continues to live in his heart, and always shall.

Tonight, April 13th, Joseph's spirits are high. He's dressed in a snazzy new suit that drained his replenished savings, but it was worth it. Opening night of his first ever gallery showing is drawing to a close. The full contents of his storage closet are on display for all to see. By every account it was a smashing success and a culmination of months of knocking on doors and showing his works to anyone remotely involved in the arts community.

His painting 'Man on Front Step' sold to a well known music producer for fifteen hundred dollars. A fortune in Joseph's eyes. He also received two offers of representation from agents whom he promised he would consider. He honestly doesn't have a clue how he'll choose or what's involved, but it's a great problem to have.

Now the gallery is nearly empty, the free drinks have been drunk and only a bit of chatter remains. After generously thanking the gallery owner who gave him his big break, as well as the folks who worked the show, Joseph makes his exit.

Stopping outside the gallery, he buttons up his jacket. Looking at the poster bearing his name next to the door, he smiles. Joseph pulls his phone from his pocket to take a photo commemorating the occasion. The prestigious Bronstein Gallery stands before him, well known for discovering and catapulting fresh new artists into prominence. He backs up enough to get the entire front of the building in the shot. He clicks and gives the picture a cursory check. Then, just before he goes to close the image on his phone, something catches his eye.

The spring air catches in his lungs and his fingers attack the tiny screen, trying to enlarge the picture. As he zooms in on the reflection in the window of the gallery, he spots himself... but he is not alone.

At his side in the reflection is a beautiful woman in a flowing white gown. Her long hair is dark and lightly curled. The face may be obscured in the dimly lit image, but clearly visible are the large iridescent wings on her back.

Joseph whips his head around wildly and spins every which way, looking for the woman in the photo. "Sara!" He cries out loudly. "Sara?!"

The street is deserted, he is alone on the sidewalk, and Sara is nowhere to be seen. When he looks back to his phone, the woman has vanished from the photo. The reflection shows him alone, holding his up phone... nothing more.

He laughs softly to himself and remembers the overwhelming feeling he had six months ago when Sara vanished from his arms.

This is not the end.

Returning to his apartment very late, Joseph is grateful not to be waylaid by Mrs. Jackson. Evidently she does sleep occasionally. Turning on the lights, the apartment is as he left it several hours ago. There is a large corkboard on one wall of the living room covered with a multitude of rough drawings and paint color tests. Nearby sits a large easel with a nearly completed painting upon it. Not a new work, but an original work, the only unfinished painting from his closet. A vision he had seen in his mind for years, virtually all his life. Walking up to it, he scrutinizes it closely.

It is a painting of woman, standing almost in profile, wearing a flowing white gown. Dark brown locks tumble luxuriantly over her shoulders. Her head is bowed and though her lavender eyes are hidden, they somehow still exude hope. There is a smile on her lips that radiates joy and love. Newly painted are two beautiful opalescent wings casually folded against her back. It is Sara, his angel. A painting started years before Joseph ever found her. And in the painting the lithe hands of Joseph's angel rest lovingly upon her noticeably round belly.

A brand new life, unlike anything before it, burgeoning within her... a bright new light in the universe.

This is not the end...

Printed in Great Britain
by Amazon